MISS SHAW AND THE DOCTOR

Sarah Shaw, on her way to take up a position as governess with Lady Fenwick, accidentally causes Dr Adam Moorcroft to be thrown from his gig and over the hedge — not an auspicious start to their relationship. When Isobel Fenwick contracts measles, Sarah moves her charges to Adam's home to protect the newborn Fenwick heir. However, tragedy strikes . . . Sarah promises she will stay as long as the girls need her. But will she be able to keep her promise?

FENELLA MILLER

◆

MISS SHAW AND THE DOCTOR

Complete and Unabridged

LINFORD
Leicester

First published in Great Britain in 2011

First Linford Edition
published 2011

British Library CIP Data

Miller, Fenella-Jane.
  Miss Shaw and the doctor. - -
(Linford romance library)
  1. Governesses- -Fiction
  2. Physicians- -Fiction.
  3. Love stories.
  4. Large type books.
  I. Title II. Series
  823.9′2–dc22

  ISBN 978–1–4448–0798–1

Published by
F. A. Thorpe (Publishing)
Anstey, Leicestershire

Set by Words & Graphics Ltd.
Anstey, Leicestershire
Printed and bound in Great Britain by
T. J. International Ltd., Padstow, Cornwall

1

'Bentley crossroads. Miss Shaw, it's time for you to alight.'

Sarah jerked awake. It was pitch dark inside the mail coach, not even a glimmer of moonlight. 'Thank you, Coachman, I am coming.' By the time she had stumbled down the steps her trunk and carpetbag were on the dirt beside the road. Before she had time to straighten her bonnet and shake out the creases from her skirts the coach had gone, leaving her alone in the middle of the night in a deserted country lane.

Her employer, Sir John Fenwick, was to have sent someone to meet her. However, she was several hours later than the time she'd put in her letter as the lead horse had cast a shoe. This had meant the coach being obliged to travel at walking pace to the next stop. It had then taken a further three hours to find a blacksmith and get the beast reshod. It was ever thus with equines, there was always something needed doing to them. Whatever minion he had sent would have returned to the squire's abode long since.

A distant church clock struck the hour; she counted carefully. It was midnight, it would not be dawn for another few hours. Thank God it was June, the weather clement. It would be no hardship to sit on something that didn't rock from side to side for a few hours. The sweet sound of nightingales came from a nearby woodland, she smiled, she was to be entertained whilst she waited. Sitting on the lumpy curved lid of the trunk became uncomfortable, it would be better on the ground using her carpetbag to lean on. Her eyes closed and she drifted asleep.

★　★　★

'Dr Moorcroft, sir, you're wanted at Bentley Manor, Lady Fenwick is unwell.'

2

Adam was wide awake and throwing on his clothes before his housekeeper had finished speaking. 'Tell them I will be with them directly. Send word to the stable to have my gig brought round.'

Less than ten minutes from his call he was on his way, his medical bag on the seat. With the lanterns bobbing on either side, he guided his horse down the country lane that would lead him to the squire's house. Lady Fenwick's fifth child was on its way, he was anxious to be with her throughout the labour. He had been against her trying for a boy, her heart was weak and the strain of delivery could prove too much for her. However, the pregnancy had been remarkably easy, when he had examined her two days ago there had been no sign of the erratic heartbeat that had characterised the other pregnancies.

There was no time for delay, he must urge his team into a canter despite their danger of doing so in the dark.

$\star$ $\star$ $\star$

3

Sarah heard the sound of rapidly approaching hooves and pushed herself upright. How kind of the squire to send someone out to look for her, she had fully expected to be waiting until the morning to be collected. She picked up her carpetbag and withdrew her handkerchief from her reticule to wipe some of the grime from her hands.

The carriage was travelling at a spanking trot, showed no sign of pulling up, the driver could not have seen her. So stepping forward, she waved her handkerchief furiously. The terrified beasts reared up, the carriage slewed sideways and the unfortunate driver sailed from his perch and vanished over the hedge.

'Oh my goodness! What have I done?' The horse, having recovered from its fright, was standing a few yards away, the outline of the carriage clearly discernible in the welcome light of the lanterns.

It was the driver she was most concerned about. Then the hedge moved and the head and shoulders of the missing man emerged. He was covered in twigs, his hair awry, and his once smart topcoat ripped from collar to tails. This was no servant, she had made a grave error of judgement. The gentleman did not look at all pleased to see her, in fact he looked furious.

'I do beg your pardon, I thought you were a servant from the Manor come to collect me.'

He drew himself up, he must be two yards in his stocking feet and every inch was quivering with rage. 'Are you run mad? Only an imbecile would leap out into the middle of the road waving her handkerchief. You are lucky we were both not killed by your stupidity.'

Sarah bristled. How could she have known the silly animal would tip its master over the hedge? She had already apologised, there was no need for him to be so unpleasant. 'If I had not done so you would not have stopped. As a gentleman I'm sure that you would not wish me to be marooned here on my own for the rest of the night.' She risked moving closer and curtsied politely. 'I am Miss Sarah Shaw, the new governess for Lady Fenwick. I have been sitting here for over two hours.'

'Dr Adam Moorcroft.' He barely nodded, he was still not ready to accept her admission of guilt with good grace. 'I suppose I shall have to give you a lift as I am going to The Manor myself.' He viewed her large trunk with disfavour. 'That will have to remain where it is until tomorrow. Bring your carpetbag. Let us hope, Miss Shaw, that my horses are not lame after your foolishness.'

'All that I possess is in that trunk, if you will not put it in your vehicle then I shall remain behind with it. Please, do not let me delay you. No doubt you are on your way to deliver Lady Fenwick's child.'

She'd expected him to pick up her trunk, however reluctantly, and toss it in the gig. He shrugged and turned his back, his parting words were not conciliatory. 'As you wish. You will come to no harm here, I shall inform them that you're waiting. Goodnight, Miss Shaw, I cannot say it was a pleasure meeting you.'

Before she could protest he jumped back into his carriage, collected the reins and vanished, like the mail coach, into the night. Sarah dropped her bag on the ground and barely restrained herself from jumping on it. The man was a monster. No gentleman would leave a lady, however humble, in the darkness on her own. If she had the misfortune to meet him again she would have something pertinent to say to him — and it would not be all polite.

Scarcely half an hour had passed before a small cart arrived from the opposite direction. Somewhat mollified, she greeted the youth holding the reins with more enthusiasm than the situation warranted. 'Thank you so much for coming out to fetch me. I cannot tell you how pleased I am to see you, I have been sitting here this age.'

'The doctor woke us up and told me

to get out here quick smart. You hop in, Miss Shaw, I'll get your trunk in the back.'

After a considerable amount of heaving and pushing the object was safely installed in the pony trap. It was now after one o'clock in the morning, Sarah prayed that her poor start in her new employment would not be held against her. No doubt the house would be fully occupied preparing for the arrival of the baby. If it was a boy this time she was certain Sir John and his wife would be so happy her tardy arrival would be forgotten.

'There, miss, all right and tight. I reckon you'd have bin there until morning if the doctor hadn't routed me out.'

'I shall remember to thank him next time we meet. What is your name?'

'Dan Smith, Miss Shaw. I'm a stable boy, I ain't been here long, only started last Michaelmas.'

By the time they arrived at their destination Sarah knew far more than she wished to about Dan and his work;

she had also discovered the last governess had left under a cloud. The boy was somewhat unclear as to why, but he was certain the young lady had not been there more than a few months before she was dismissed.

Full of foreboding she clambered out of the vehicle when it rolled to a stop behind the house.

'My trunk can remain where it is until morning. Thank you again for your assistance, Dan.' With a cheery wave he drove off leaving her to find her own way in. As was to be expected there were lights throughout the house, if she knocked on the side door someone was bound to let her in.

'Lawks, there you are, Miss Shaw. We was wondering what had happened to you. I'm Betty, your maid, I've to show you to your room.' The woman curtsied and all but snatched the bag from Sarah's hand. 'This way, we'll take the back stairs, too much going on round the front.'

Even these stairs had burning sconces,

no expense was spared in this establishment. It was a good sign, in her opinion, when staff were treated well. Betty led her through the twisting passageways, up several narrow staircases and out into a spacious corridor.

'Here we are, miss, her ladyship insisted the candles were lit. It's been a mite difficult since Miss Reynolds left three weeks ago.' Betty shook her head before continuing in little more than a whisper. 'I'm warning you, miss, the little girls look like angels but they're not. I daren't say no more, more than my job's worth.' She pushed open a door and stepped aside. 'Here you are, Cook has sent you up a nice supper tray.' She grinned. 'More like a midnight feast, you're lucky everyone's up because of the baby, otherwise you'd not have got in. Mr Foster, the butler, locks up at ten o'clock sharp when the master and mistress are home.'

Sarah stepped into her chamber, there must be more than half a dozen candles burning; such luxury. This was her private parlour, well appointed and of a good size. The furnishings were fresh and dainty, it looked like somewhere she could be happy. 'Thank you for bringing me up here Betty, I shall manage very well now that I *am* here. I'm sure you have other duties to attend to.'

'Lawks, Miss Shaw, didn't I say? I'm to look after you. Your bed chamber's through that door, if you'd care to give me your bag I shall lay out your night things whilst you eat your supper.' Under the crisp white cloth was a veritable feast indeed. A warm meat pasty, fresh bread and cheese, chutneys and pickles and a dish of hothouse peaches. To drink with it was a jug of freshly made lemonade and a pot of piping hot coffee. It had been so long since she had eaten she was sharp set and finished everything. Wiping her lips on the napkin she leant back in her chair with a sigh of contentment. She was going to love it here, she would completely disregard Betty's improper comment about her young charges. It was up to her to bring order into their lives, to restore harmony in the schoolroom.

Bidding goodnight to the friendly maid, she removed her soiled outer garments and released her corset. With a sigh of relief she tossed the hideous garment aside. Mama had once shown her a book of fashion plates from years ago when all ladies of quality wore their gowns high waisted, it must have been a comfortable fashion.

Quickly washing in the pitcher of warm water so thoughtfully provided she slipped on her nightgown and returned to her bedroom. She wasn't sure if she should get into bed, she was so fatigued she feared she would not wake up in time to start her duties. She took her responsibilities seriously, with Lady Fenwick confined it was up to her to take care of the four little girls.

Perhaps she would risk it, she had five hours until she had to rise. In her previous employment she had been expected to be in the schoolroom to supervise breakfast. It was rare that she got to her bed before eleven, there were lessons to prepare for the next day as well as taking care of her own laundry and mending in what little spare time she had.

It had been a great relief when the family had decided to move to Scotland, this gave her the opportunity to hand in her notice and seek fresh employment. The agency she had used had welcomed her, and her excellent references, and there had been several jobs available. Taking care of four girls aged between four and nine years of age had appealed to her. It was a ready-made class, there was so much more one could do to make lessons interesting when there was more than one child being taught.

★ ★ ★

The delicious aroma of chocolate woke her. Sarah pushed herself upright and stared in delight at the tray left on the bedside table. She was certainly not going to go hungry in the establishment. A small ormolu clock on the mantelshelf struck seven times. Heavens, what a poor start, she should have been in the schoolroom preparing for her charges an hour ago. She tumbled out of bed and ran across to the dressing room almost colliding with Betty who was gathering up the garments she had worn yesterday.

'I am so late. I should have been . . . '

'No need to worry, miss, Miss Reynolds wasn't expected to be in the schoolroom until eight thirty. I didn't like to wake you when I brought in your chocolate, you run back to bed and have your breakfast. When I've finished hanging up your clothes your bath will be ready.'

It would seem that she was to be treated like a member of the family and not a servant. She had not met either Sir John or Lady Fenwick, the job offer had been made on her letter of application and references alone. She was certain this job would be far more to her liking than the previous one.

As she sipped her chocolate and nibbled on a soft morning roll liberally spread with honey, she called out. 'Betty, has the baby arrived yet?'

'No, but it should be any moment now. If it's a boy this time, my word, there'll be some celebrations.'

Word came from downstairs that the new arrival was the much wanted boy. What a good start to her time here, she would make the day a happy one, a brief introductory lesson and then the remainder of the day would be devoted to entertainment in honour of the girls' baby brother.

After the unusual luxury of a bath Sarah made her way to the schoolroom. This was on the same floor as her apartment; her rooms were tucked away in a corner. The schoolroom and nurseries were in the main part of the building facing the park, all that was required of her was to cross the hallway in which the children's staircase was located and she was at her destination.

It was a grey day, the sky heavy, she hoped it didn't rain until she had had time to take the children outside. She paused to check her reflection in the window. Her collars and cuffs were sparkling white, her dark green gown uncreased, her hair neatly coiled at the back of her neck. Satisfied, she walked briskly to the schoolroom door, it had been left slightly ajar but she could hear no sound of the girls inside.

Stepping in she discovered she had arrived before her pupils. Excellent, this would give her time to get out the slates and find the other items she needed for the morning lesson. The desks were set out neatly, two in front and two behind. The blackboard and easel was well supplied with chalk, the ink pots were full and the pens had sharpened nibs. There was a globe, a bookcase full of both factual and fiction books and in a cupboard were paints and brushes and paper.

All that was required were her pupils. She had prepared a welcome gift for each, a pretty watercolour, their names encircled by roses in the centre of each picture. Elizabeth, the youngest, was four years of age, upon hers were rabbits. She put this on the desk nearest to the front. Charlotte, who was two years her senior, had cats on hers. Isobel and Lorna, twins had just celebrated their ninth birthday, and had horses on their paintings.

She checked the fob watch pinned to her bodice. The girls were tardy, it was already three minutes past the time they were expected to be in the schoolroom. She would not stand and wait but go and find them. Her letter of appointment had been specific, it was her task to restore order in their lives.

Betty had explained where the girls' chambers were situated. There was no sound coming from behind the first door, she would not knock, it was her right to enter as she pleased. Again the door was slightly open, she pushed it firmly. A slight noise above her head made her glance upwards. Too late. She was bombarded by a miscellany of books and other hard objects which had been balanced across the opening. Screams of laughter greeted this unpleasant experience.

For a moment Sarah swayed in the doorway, the impact of the books on her head making her dizzy, and the pain bringing tears to her eyes. She gritted her teeth. She would not retreat in disarray; if she did, the pattern would be set and her charges would have ascendancy. Stepping forward, rigid with anger, she viewed the culprits. Under her stern stare the giggles faded. She addressed Isobel, as it was obvious that she had been the instigator of this unkind prank.

'Isobel, today was to have been a time of celebration for you and your sisters. Instead it will be spent at your desks. I doubt that this silliness will be considered a good idea by the time you are allowed to retire.' She pointed to the door. 'In silence, if you please, make your way to the schoolroom.'

They trooped past her, she almost relented when she heard the little ones crying, but she must punish them all. Although she was angry, she had no wish to cause dissension between the children. A nervous nursery maid was hovering outside the door wringing her hands. Sarah pointed to the scattered objects. 'Get this cleaned up. Have someone from the nursery come to me in the schoolroom immediately.'

The girl nodded, but had the good sense to make no comment. It was too late to remove the gifts she had made for the girls, perhaps seeing them would make them realise how unkind they had been. The under-nursery maid arrived, a girl with an unsmiling countenance.

'Kindly supervise the girls. They have work to do, it will be done in silence. I shall not be long.' Sarah paused at the door, every blonde head was industriously scribbling on their slates. Even little Beth was attempting to copy her name. As she turned to leave Isobel looked up. The hate on the girl's face shocked her. Why should this child feel so strongly about someone she had only just met?

Somehow she stumbled to her apartment. Her vision was blurred; if she did not lie down she would drop to the floor in a swoon. Betty greeted her, her outrage barely contained.

'My word, what have those naughty children done now?'

From a distance Sarah heard her maid clucking sympathetically, then she sank gratefully on to the day bed and her world went black.

2

Adam was on his way out when the housekeeper stopped him. 'Sir, I beg your pardon, but there has been an incident in the schoolroom. Miss Shaw has been injured.'

'I shall come at once, tell me what happened.'

'Something fell on her head. She was able to return to her room but is now unconscious.'

His hand clenched around the handle of his medical bag. Head injuries were the worst, it was often impossible to gauge the seriousness of the injury. The young woman he'd met a few hours ago had not endeared herself to him, however, he was saddened to think she had met with an accident so soon after her arrival.

He had been to the nursery floor on more than one occasion to attend one or other of the girls when they had succumbed to various childhood ailments. Mrs Taylor led him to the rear of the house and into a pretty parlour. Lying comatose on a *chaise-longue* was his patient. He could see at once there was a livid bruise on her right temple.

Dropping to his knees beside her he checked her pulse; thank God it was strong and regular. 'Fetch me a basin of cold water and clean cloths.' These arrived at his side immediately. Folding the square into a pad he immersed it in the cold water and then held it gently against the bruise.

Miss Shaw stirred and woke up. A peculiar sensation rippled down his spine as he stared into the most amazing eyes he had ever encountered. They were the colour of amethyst, flecked with gold. She did not recognize him at first, then as her senses returned so too did her memory. Her remarkable eyes darkened and her mouth tightened. She was not pleased to see him.

What was *this* man doing in her apartment? 'Dr Moorcroft, I did not ask for your services. I received a bump on the head and felt a little faint for a few moments.' He uncoiled from his position on the floor to stand looking down at her, a strange expression on his face. 'As you can see I am almost fully recovered.'

'I believe I am best qualified to decide if you are recovered or not, Miss Shaw.' He turned to Betty. 'How long was your mistress unconscious?'

'Five minutes, no longer, sir. You wouldn't believe what happened, those . . . '

'Enough, Betty. Dr Moorcroft does not need to delay here longer. He has been awake all night and no doubt wishes to return to his own home.' Sarah had no desire for word of this escapade to go downstairs.

'Miss Shaw, it will be a simple matter to make enquiries elsewhere. Kindly tell

23

me how you received this injury.' His lips softened, he almost smiled, and she felt her antagonism melting. He was an attractive gentleman when he wasn't frowning.

'Some books fell on my head, it was an accident. Now, Dr Moorcroft, thank you for coming to my aid but I must return to my duties.'

His expression changed, he was frowning again. 'Good grief, am I to understand that one of your charges was responsible? They could have killed you. I shall inform Sir John . . . '

Sarah swung her feet to the floor and pushed herself upright. 'You shall do no such thing, sir. I have no wish for this day of happy celebration to be spoiled in this way. I shall deal with it myself.'

Was it admiration she saw flicker across his face? He nodded. 'As you wish, Miss Shaw. I suppose there is little point in me telling you to remain where you are?'

'None at all. No doubt I shall have a nasty headache, but my vision is clear and I do not believe I have a concussion. Please excuse me, Dr Moorcroft, I have been away too long from my charges.'

He seemed reluctant to stand aside. 'I am returning this evening to visit Lady Fenwick and the baby. I shall call in to see you at the same time.'

Sarah was tempted to argue, but thought better of it. 'Very well, my duties in the schoolroom should be completed by six o'clock.' She sailed past him and was at the schoolroom door before he could remonstrate.

Four heads swivelled to stare at her. Elizabeth and Charlotte burst into noisy tears, Lorna glanced nervously at her sister and Isobel smirked. The girl who had been left to supervise in her absence looked equally disturbed. Then Sarah recalled the lump on her forehead. She must reassure them that she was not seriously injured.

'Elizabeth, Charlotte, there's no need to cry. I am perfectly well apart from a bump on the head. I hope this will be a lesson to you all, I could have been gravely injured by your prank.' She looked at each one in turn, and even Isobel seemed uncomfortable. 'I am sure that Sir John would be most displeased that I was greeted in this way.'

Isobel jumped to her feet sending her slate smashing to the boards. 'Oh, please, Miss Shaw, do not tell Papa. He threatened to send me away to school after the last time.'

'Sit down, Isobel. I have no intention of informing your parents today, but only because of the arrival of your little brother. I shall not hesitate if anything of this nature occurs a second time.'

The youngest girls sniffed noisily. Sarah wondered if tears were a tactic they often employed to deflect punishment. Lorna smiled, it was the first genuine expression of friendship from any of them. 'I shall inspect your handwriting, if it is not to my satisfaction you will do it again. Isobel, pick up your broken slate and fetch yourself a new one. You must repeat the exercise.'

They all looked so miserable she wanted to relent, gather them to her and say they were forgiven. But she must be firm, she needed this position and had a sinking feeling that, despite their apparent docility, for some reason she was not welcome in the school-room.

In silence she checked each slate. All had completed their tasks well enough.

'Good, I now wish you, Lorna, to transfer the passage to your copybook. Isobel, when you have finished writing on your slate you will do the same. Charlotte, you will write your first sentence and then illustrate appropriately. Elizabeth, I wish you to copy your name as it is on the cards that I gave you and then draw a suitable picture.'

The chorus of 'Yes, Miss Shaw,' was subdued and they settled to their task obediently. At ten thirty she heard the sound of rattling crockery next-door. The children's mid-morning snack had arrived. It was time to relax the atmosphere a little, one and a half hours of working in complete silence was more than enough, especially for the little ones.

'You may put down your pens and pencils, children. We shall take a break for twenty minutes and then return to do some mathematics until luncheon.'

* * *

So the remainder of the day passed uneventfully. Beth, Lottie and Lorna had all apologised for their part in the unpleasantness and she had forgiven them. However, Isobel still remained aloof. She was scrupulously polite but permanently watchful. At three o'clock Sarah decided the children had done their penance.

'Girls, as you have been so well-behaved you can put down your sewing. I have arranged for a picnic tea to be prepared. I had hoped you would be able to take me out into the park, but it is far too wet for that.'

'Miss Shaw, please can we still have the picnic? We could take it to the stables, it would be dry there.'

Sarah shuddered at the thought. 'Lorna, my dear, I think it would be lovely to visit the horses another time, but not today.'

Beth threw her arms around Sarah's knees. 'Please, can we have a picnic? I've never had one.'

'I have an idea, why don't we take it into the attics? We could pretend to be explorers, play a game of hide and go seek. But first you must change into your oldest clothes, it would not do to spoil your pretty gowns.'

Her suggestion was received with squeals of delight; even Isobel allowed herself a little smile. Nancy and Jo, the two nursery maids, were dispatched to the kitchen to fetch the food. The girls rushed off to change leaving Sarah to enjoy a few moments' solitude. Her head was aching abominably, the last thing she wanted was to racket about in a dusty attic, but the children must come first. She wanted the day to end on a good note, and for her charges to return to the nursery feeling happy with their new governess.

* * *

'Mrs Taylor, I wish to see Miss Shaw before I leave. I have looked everywhere upstairs in the nursery wing and cannot locate her or the children. I understood that her duties would be completed by this time.'

The housekeeper curtsied. 'Indeed, Dr Moorcroft, that had always been the case.' The woman smiled. 'However, today Miss Shaw has taken the children into the attics to have a picnic. They are up there playing hide and go seek.'

Shaking his head in disbelief, Adam was in two minds. Miss Shaw was obviously fully recovered and in no need of his services, but something prompted him to take the stairs that would lead him to the attics. She was an extraordinary young lady, he could think of no one else of his acquaintance who would take a picnic to such a place.

The sound of childish laughter echoed down the stairwell, the game was obviously still in full swing. Would his appearance be viewed with dis-favour? It sounded like fun, it was far too long since he'd had any himself.

He stooped through the narrow door and held his candlestick aloft. The flicker of light came from further into the roof space, it was possible to see without a candle so he blew it out. Far easier to negotiate the old trunks, items of furniture and piles of other unwanted debris, with both his hands free. It had gone strangely silent, then he heard one of the older girls counting out loud. Before he could announce his presence Miss Shaw hurtled from the room ahead and straight into his arms.

Instinctively he closed them, hoping to keep his balance and save them both from a tumble. They rocked perilously for a few seconds, all would have been well if she had not tried to step away.

'Release me this instant, Dr Moorcroft,' she hissed indignantly.

Her sudden movement unbalanced him and they toppled sideways. Somehow he managed to twist his body so that he took the brunt of the fall. They landed between two battered armchairs, effectively jamming his arms making it impossible for him to move. Miss Shaw was squashed beside him. She was rigid within his grip.

'I say, Dr Moorcroft, are we playing Sardines now?'

He glanced upwards to see two little faces smiling down at him. Miss Shaw recovered her composure far quicker than he.

'Indeed, Beth and Lottie, we are. Quickly now, scramble in with us. Lorna will be upon us at any moment.'

The children needed no second bidding and he found himself the mattress upon which three bodies rested. The stifled giggles coming from the girls relaxed the tension. Soon he was having difficulty controlling his mirth, he could feel Miss Shaw quivering with suppressed laughter. Somehow the disaster had been turned into a highly enjoyable occasion.

Lorna walked right past them but hurried back when one of the girls sneezed loudly. 'Found you! I didn't know that Dr Moorcroft was playing. Come on Beth, Lottie, help me find Isobel.'

* * *

Sarah scrambled up as soon as the children had removed themselves, relieved it was too dark for Dr Moorcroft to see her scarlet cheeks. At least Lorna had not thought they were doing anything immodest; she was sure that Lady Fenwick would not view the incident in the same way. He was right behind her. Why didn't he speak?

'Dr Moorcroft, I do beg your pardon for involving you in the children's game.

However, I must enquire what you are doing in the attics in the first place?'

His rich, deep chuckle filled the space. 'Believe it or not, Miss Shaw, I had come to check if you were fully recovered from your accident.'

'In the attics? That is beyond the call of duty, sir.' She couldn't prevent her lips curving. He was a most unusual gentleman, that was for sure.

'Shall we assist with the search for the missing child? It sounds as if the other three are having difficulty locating her.'

Sarah had been thinking just that herself. On previous occasions Isobel's hiding places had been ingenious, but none had taken so long to discover. 'I shall ring the bell, I brought one up here with me for such an occasion. They all know it means the end of the game and they must return at once to me. I have the picnic hamper in the next room.'

Sarah had the brass bell in her hand. The tinkle reverberated throughout the attics; immediately there was the sound of little feet running towards her. First came the two littlest, close behind was Lorna, but Isobel was not with them. Frowning she rang the bell again and listened. She could hear nothing above the girls' chatter. 'Please, girls, can you be silent for a moment. I'm becoming concerned Isobel might have become lost. If we are quiet we will hear her calling.'

She called the child's name and still there was no response. Dr Moorcroft called — surely Isobel would have heard him wherever she was. 'Nancy, take the girls down to the nursery. Nanny will be expecting them. Dr Moorcroft and I will find Miss Isobel and bring her to you.'

If this had happened this morning she would have thought the girl deliberately hiding in order to cause trouble, but during the past few hours things had improved between them. Isobel was still wary, for some reason, but more than once she had smiled with genuine affection. Now she was convinced something was preventing the girl from responding. 'I am concerned that Isobel is in difficulties. I apologise for assuming you will help me look for her, you must have more important duties to attend to than looking for a little girl in an attic.'

'Of course I shall stay until we find Isobel. We must take candles and search separately. Can you remember in which direction she went?'

Sarah shook her head. 'Not this way, but there are a dozen other rooms she could be in. I shall take the ones closest to the window, if you would be so kind as to search in the other direction?'

After ten minutes Isobel had still not been found. Sarah held her candlestick high and looked around the small room she was in, it was empty apart from two trunks and an old fire screen. She was about to leave when a slight sound attracted her attention. It came inside the trunk pushed closest to the wall.

Her heart was thudding, she took a deep breath and called softly. 'Isobel, sweetheart, is that you?' The sound again, this time she recognized it as a sob. Rushing forward she threw back the lid and saw the girl lying with her eyes squeezed shut in the small space. The trunk was too deep for her to reach down and lift Isobel from the floor. From the smell it was apparent the poor little thing had had an accident.

'Dr Moorcroft, Dr Moorcroft, I have found her, please come at once to help,' Stretching down she gently stroked the girl's hand. 'Don't worry, my love, we shall soon have you out of here and clean and warm in your bed.'

Isobel's fingers gripped hers but she said nothing. Then pounding footsteps announced the arrival of the doctor. 'She's in here, the lid must have dropped closed on her and she couldn't open it.'

Strong hands gripped her around the waist and lifted her sideways as if she weighed no more than a pillow. 'Stand aside, Miss Shaw, I shall carry her downstairs.'

With Isobel in his arms he straightened, in the flickering light the candle she could see his expression was tender, he was murmuring quietly to the terrified child. 'I shall take her to her chamber, Miss Shaw, the nursery maid will soon have her fully restored.'

He took her into the small room adjacent to the older girls' bed chamber where Nancy was waiting to strip Isobel and lift her into a waiting bath tub. He smiled at the trembling girl and strode off without so much as a nod to Sarah.

'Isobel, I'm so sorry we didn't find you sooner. I walked past the trunk before I heard you call.'

The child's pale blue eyes were huge in her ashen face. 'Oh, Miss Shaw, please do not tell Papa that I have caused so much trouble today.' Sarah dropped to her knees beside the child and gathered her into her arms. 'My love, I promise you he shall hear nothing from me. We will put today behind us, and start afresh tomorrow. What do you say?'

'Thank you, Miss Shaw, I promise I shall be good in future.'

'I am relieved to hear you say so, my dear. I shall leave you to have your bath in peace. The weather is improving, had you noticed the sun's shining now? Tomorrow afternoon you and your sisters must show me around the park.'

Leaving Isobel in the capable hands of a maid she returned to the nursery where she could hear the other children laughing and talking. 'Girls, Isobel had become shut fast in a trunk. She is having a bath and will then be able to join you for nursery tea. I am retiring to my own apartment, I look forward to seeing you at half past eight in the schoolroom.'

Beth ran over and tugged at her hand. 'Miss Shaw, lessons don't start until nine o'clock.'

'No, my dear, *my* lessons start at half an hour earlier. Goodnight, girls, I have had an interesting day.'

She was scarcely inside her sitting room when a footman appeared with a message demanding that she come down at once to speak to Sir John in the drawing-room. She had been expecting the summons, after all she had yet to meet her new employer. No doubt she would have to wait to meet the lady of the house until after her confinement was over. The liveried servant stopped outside and politely opened one of the double doors.

It was only as she dipped in a low curtsy she remembered she had not done anything to repair her appearance. She would be covered in cobwebs, there was a wet patch on her skirt from Isobel's accident, and she could feel her neatly arranged chignon was unravelling at the back of her neck. No doubt the livid bruise was visible also.

3

Slowly she raised her eyes to find a tall, spare, gentleman in his forties staring at her his eyebrows raised in puzzlement. 'Miss Shaw, I do apologise for calling you down so abruptly. Would it be more convenient to speak to me tomorrow?'

Sarah smiled ruefully. 'I fear the damage is already done, Sir John. I have been playing in the attic with the girls, I beg your pardon for not attending to matters before I came down. I can assure you, sir, that I am normally neat as a pin.'

'I intended to ask you to sit down, but perhaps, in the circumstances you will excuse me if I do not extend that courtesy. Now, Miss Shaw, I'm sure that you have heard I have my son. What you will not have heard, and I do not wish the girls to know, that their mama is not at all well. She has a weak heart. We were advised against attempting to have an heir, but we are both glad we did so.'

'I congratulate you on the arrival of your much longed for son. I shall keep the girls occupied so they do not notice they are not allowed to visit. Please convey my sympathies and best wishes to Lady Fenwick.'

'I shall do that, Miss Shaw. However, my wife is most insistent that you come and see her tomorrow. She is an overindulgent mother, much prefers to have the children with her all day and not in the care of a governess. No doubt you have been told that you are the third such person to be employed in this establishment this year.' He frowned, and extracted his fob watch. For a sober man he had a remarkably flamboyant waistcoat, it contrasted strangely with his dark tailcoat, white shirt and neatly tied cravat.

He glanced up and caught her staring. She felt the blood rush to her cheeks. Instead of being offended at her temerity he smiled, it made him look far less austere. 'I know, Miss Shaw, it is a hideous garment. However, Lady Fenwick made it with her own fair hands and I would not wear anything else.'

What a delightful gentleman he was, he obviously adored his wife and children. The house was a happy one, she was determined to remain here whatever scrapes Isobel led her into. 'Sir John, when would her ladyship like to see me? I intend to start lessons half an hour earlier, this means we can eat our luncheon at midday and have the afternoon for fresh air and exercise.'

His smile had vanished, he was looking at her through narrowed eyes. 'Miss Shaw, how did you come by that bruise on your forehead?'

She swallowed nervously. 'An accident with some books. I can assure you, Sir John it looks far worse than it is.'

'If you are sure there is nothing I should know, then I shall not detain you. You have had a long day.' He called as she was at the door. 'I quite forgot, you have not told me why you were not waiting at the crossroads at the appointed time. Lady Fenwick will wish to know.' When she had explained he nodded sympathetically. 'Most unfortunate. Let us hope that your next few days are less eventful for all our sakes. Come to Lady Fenwick's apartment at ten thirty. I shall send a footman to fetch you.'

∗ ∗ ∗

The girls appeared on time next morning and even Isobel seemed inclined to co-operate. Sarah had been in the schoolroom since seven preparing individual work programmes. Even the twins required separate tasks as Isobel was far more advanced academically than her quieter sister.

She had dressed with particular attention to her appearance that morning, arranging her hair so that several curls fell over the livid bruise. She was almost sure it would be unnoticed by Lady Fenwick. 'Now, girls, Nancy shall sit with you whilst you have your snack. I'm certain that your Mama will love the card you have finished for her.'

She held up the item for them to admire. Their little brother was to be named John after their father, this had been drawn on to a rectangle of card and then each child had added their own illustrations. Isobel and Lorna had been given the task of painting in the letters. On the reverse they had all signed their names.

'It's so pretty, Miss Shaw, I think Mama will love it.'

'I'm certain that she will, Lorna. I shall tell her how hard you are working and how pleased I am to find such industrious pupils. There, I hear the tray next door. You may be excused. Lessons will resume when I return.'

Isobel hung back letting her sisters run ahead into the nursery. 'Miss Shaw, I want to see my mama, take me with you.'

'I'm sorry, my dear, not today. As soon as she is rested you will all be asked to come down and meet the new arrival.'

The child scowled, and for a moment Sarah thought she would refuse to accept this information. 'I am the oldest, Miss Shaw. Mama loves me best, she will want to see *me* even if the others don't go.' Her blonde ringlets bounced on her shoulders as she ran to join her sisters. Sarah sighed, it seemed as if the temporary truce was over.

Lady Fenwick was much younger than her husband, a pretty, older version of her daughters. There was a worrying blueness about her lips. Sarah prayed that this pregnancy had not proved too much. She was greeted with a tired smile.

'Welcome, Miss Shaw, how are my girls? I do so wish to see Isobel, she will be fretting if she is kept away from me for long.'

Sarah dipped politely and moved closer to the enormous tester bed.

There was no sign of the cradle, the baby was obviously being cared for in the nursery. 'All your daughters are well, they have sent you a small gift.' She passed over the card waiting for the exclamations of joy. 'Ah, so pretty, you will thank them for me, won't you, Miss Shaw?'

Lady Fenwick's eyes drooped, it was time to go. Quietly Sarah moved towards the door, as she was opening it her employer spoke again. 'You must think me an unnatural parent, to be talking only of Isobel. But she was so tiny when she was born, we feared she would not survive. I carried her around in my bosom, fed her from a teaspoon every few minutes. Against all the odds my little girl thrived, but she is not quite the same as the others.' Sarah held her breath, she knew what was coming next. 'I'm sure an intelligent young woman like yourself will already have noticed she can be a trifle . . . a little . . . unbalanced sometimes.'

Sarah ran back to the bed and

impulsively clasped Lady Fenwick's cold hands. 'My lady, I understand exactly, now that I know I shall make every effort to help Isobel.'

'Thank you, my dear, I do so hope I can rely on your discretion if any unfortunate incidents do occur. My husband does not fully understand the problem, I dare not explain it in case he thinks my darling Isobel should be sent away, that she is not safe to stay at home.'

'I give you my word, Lady Fenwick, Sir John will hear nothing untoward from my lips. Please do not distress yourself, rest now, I will not disturb you further. When you are better I shall send Isobel to you first, and then the others.'

When she reached the nursery floor she found an unexpected visitor. 'Good morning, Dr Moorcroft, I did not think to see you again so soon.'

This time he bowed slightly, as he raised his head she could not help but observe that one eye was green the other brown. Her expression must have shown her surprise.

'I know, most unusual isn't it? All the males in my family are so afflicted, fortunately it does not affect our vision. Now, Miss Shaw, I should like to talk to you.' He gestured towards the padded window seat the far end of the spacious corridor. 'Shall we sit there?'

He waited until she was settled before joining her, he sat at the far end leaving a suitable distance between them. 'I have just been to see Lady Fenwick, she does not look well. She also told me about Isobel's problems and the cause of them. It explains why she is so different from the other three I . . .'

'I'm sorry, Miss Shaw, to interrupt you, but things are not as you have been told. Lady Fenwick wishes to believe that Isobel's unkind behaviour is because of something that happened in her infancy. I have made extensive enquiries, and it seems Isobel was a perfectly sweet child, no different from her twin when she was small.'

Shocked by his bluntness Sarah shook her head. 'Then I don't understand, why is she the way she is today? Did she suffer a head injury of some sort? I have heard that this can change a person's character.'

'Indeed it can. However, in this case it is merely overindulgence that has encouraged the child to use her intelligence to manipulate those around her. The previous two governesses were driven away not only by Isobel's spitefulness, but by the fact her mother always takes her side. Lady Fenwick cannot accept the fact that it is her fault her daughter has turned out so badly.'

Enough was enough. Sarah surged to her feet and stared down at him with dislike. 'I cannot believe I am hearing such balderdash from a man of medicine. Good heavens, sir, Isobel is only nine years old, how can you say she has 'turned out badly'? Being spoilt is not an incurable illness! With gentle discipline and guidance she will learn to curb her rashness and consider the outcome before embarking on a reckless or unkind act.'

By the end of her tirade he was on his feet, his jaw slack and his eyes wide. 'Well, Miss Shaw, you have certainly put me firmly in my place. I'm not sure that I believe you. Did you not know that the Franciscan monks have stated that if they have a child until he is seven years of age, he will be their acolyte for life?'

'No, I had not heard that. However, they are talking of something entirely different, they are talking of beliefs not behaviour, are they not? Now, if you will excuse me, sir, I must return to the schoolroom.'

She nodded frostily, she was not sure she could like a gentleman who was prepared to dismiss a child as incurably damaged, when all she needed was love and guidance to restore her natural goodness.

* * *

During the next two days she paid particular attention to Isobel, correcting the child whenever she showed signs of recalcitrance and then offering her a choice of activities so that it was harder for her to refuse outright to do as she was bid. So pleased was she with her progress that when Isobel made a suggestion she was prepared to listen to it.

'Miss Shaw, there is to be a fair on the green tomorrow to celebrate midsummer's day. There are horse and pony races, stilt walkers, fire eaters and lots of other things. We have never been, Mama does not like such events, do you think you could take us?'

'I shall send a note to Lady Fenwick, and if she has no objection then I should be delighted to take you. I did not intend for you to do lessons on Saturday afternoons. I was going to suggest that we took a picnic to the lake, but going to the fair sounds far more exciting.'

When she saw the child's triumphant

smile she had serious doubts about her consent. Maybe it would be better to not send the note, pretend to the children that their mother had refused her permission? This would be deceitful, against everything she held to be important. She must write the letter and abide by whatever answer she received.

Isobel was a bruising rider, Lorna did not enjoy the sport so this was one activity the girls didn't share. Whilst Isobel was away with the groom on her pony Sarah took the other three for a ramble in the woods. The bluebells were over, but the grass was carpeted with other delightful specimens they could pick and take back to the schoolroom to identify.

Dr Moorcroft had visited twice a day, the news from the sickroom was more encouraging, hopefully the girls would be able to go down and meet their new brother and see their Mama before the week was over. She wasn't sure if she was glad or disappointed that she had not spoken to him herself.

Despite her every effort she found herself thinking about him for more often than was proper. There was something about him, not just his remarkable appearance, that intrigued her. He was not in the common way, had brought modern medicine to Bentley when he'd arrived, so Betty had told her. Why was he not married with small children of his own? Her lips curved, she was forced to admit she was pleased he *was* a single gentleman.

The response from Lady Fenwick was an enthusiastic agreement. With some reluctance Sarah relayed the information to the two nursery maids. 'Tomorrow, girls, we shall be going to Bentley to see the fair. Have either of you been before and able to tell me what to expect?'

Nancy clapped in excitement. 'Are we to go with you, miss? I've not been since I've been working here, it's an annual event, the children will love it.'

'It's quite safe? I never been to such a

thing myself, had always thought undesirables would mingle with the crowd and steal one's belongings.'

'Never you mind, Miss Shaw, Nancy and I will take good care of you. If you ask for Bill and Tommy to come with us, no one will take liberties with your purse, not with them around.'

'Are Tommy and Bill grooms, or indoor servants? Have I met them, do you think?'

The girls exchanged knowing glances. 'Bill's under coachman here, we're walking out. Tommy's a groom, he's Nancy's young man. The mistress is quite happy for us to be courting, we shall be wed when a cottage comes vacant on the estate.'

'In that case, I shall certainly ask for them to come. Lady Fenwick has sent a purse full of coins for the girls to spend. We are to take the gig, will there be room for us all inside such a vehicle?'

'The little ones can sit on our laps, Miss Isobel and Miss Lorna can sit with you. It'll be a bit of a squeeze, miss, but it isn't far to the village green.'

The enthusiasm of the two nursery maids reassured Sarah that the excursion would be one they would all enjoy. The screams of delight when she informed her pupils that they would be going the next day added to her own excitement. 'You must give me your word that you will not wander off on your own. Beth and Lottie you will hold hands with Nancy and Jo at all times, is that clear?'

The girls bobbed up and down nodding vigorously. 'We promise, don't we, Beth?' Beth giggled and took her thumb from her mouth long enough to agree.

Sarah turned to the older two. 'Isobel, Lorna, you will remain with me. I do not require you to hold my hand, you are old enough to be trusted to do what you're told. Do I have your promise?'

Immediately Lorna beamed. 'I promise, Miss Shaw. I shall be too scared to go anywhere on my own, I don't much like crowds. I can't catch my breath when I'm squashed in.'

Isobel elbowed her sister scornfully. 'You're a baby, I like fairs, especially the little booths and caravans which sell trinkets.'

Sarah felt a moment's disquiet. 'I wasn't aware that you had ever attended such an event, Isobel?'

'I have seen what's there from the carriage when we passed one year. I was with Mama, we had been on a morning call, none of you came with us.'

Lessons were abandoned for the morning, her charges were far too restless to settle. Instead she took them to the impressive library which ran the length of the house on the first floor. They were given the task of finding pictures of the wildflowers they had collected the previous day. This occupied them until it was time to return to the nursery floor and get ready to leave.

The smart back and gold gig was waiting outside, two uniformed servants ready to escort them. She saw at once why Nancy had said they would be safe from molestation, both men were stoutly built and more than able to keep the girls safe. It was a worrying responsibility going out on a jaunt of this sort, she prayed that Isobel would keep her word and not do anything outrageous.

It was a glorious day, not a cloud in the sky, they would all need the protection of their straw bonnets this afternoon. She smoothed down a fold of her best gown, it was leaf green Indian cotton, and had a most unusual pattern of small birds and flowers woven into it. She had made a ribbon to go around her bonnet from the scraps. In this ensemble she felt more like a lady than a servant.

The carriage bowled through the village, it looked prosperous and well cared for. There were carts and carriages in the High Street, a hand-some market place and a haberdasher's, a milliner's, a general stores and one or two smaller establishments which could be selling anything from ironmongery to second-hand clothes. There was also a fine coaching inn, she was certain she could send her letters from there.

Several heads turned as they passed, the carriage was obviously well known to the inhabitants. She saw many substantial dwellings, a row of freshly whitewashed cottages and then the carriage slowed as it headed towards the far side where a large green was situated.

Even Isobel was chattering unreservedly about the treats to come. One thing they all wished to see was the Punch and Judy show, so this was where they would head as soon as they arrived. 'Miss Shaw, shall we go and see any of the races? It's ever such good fun, they have an enclosure specially for the smart folk, it'll be safe enough in there.'

Sarah wasn't sure about horse and pony races, her papa had been most outspoken about the evils of gambling and drink. She rather feared that both would be involved in such a pursuit. 'I do not like equines of any sort, so we will not watch those today. I am looking forward to seeing fire eaters, do you think there will be any such people?'

The girls were still bubbling over with excitement when the gig joined a long queue of like-minded vehicles heading for the entertainment. Several carriages had children in them, some waved and called out and Isobel and Lorna waved back. Seeing so many other families on their way to the fair removed the last of Sarah's fears. She relaxed and began to enjoy herself.

Eventually Bill found a suitable space and Tommy jumped down from the box and came round to let down the steps. No sooner had they descended than Lorna grabbed her hand. 'Look, Miss Shaw, see who it is coming to speak to us.'

Sarah couldn't help smiling. 'Good afternoon, Dr Moorcroft, I did not expect to see you here today.'

'Did you not? I have come to watch the races, no doubt you and the children will wish to do so. Allow me to escort you to the enclosure.'

Without a by your leave he slid her arm through his, grinning down at the four girls as he did so. 'Come along, young ladies, the first pony race is about to begin. I'm sure that we can pick a winner between us.'

The two nursemaids positively bristled with excitement, their young men exchanged happy glances. The four girls bounced up and down as eager for the treat as the rest of them. Sarah did not have the heart to disappoint, so nodded to her unwanted escort. 'I do not wish to get too close.'

The spectacle of grown men galloping around the enormous green was far more engrossing than she had expected. At the second race she was jumping up and down and calling for her favourite as loudly as everyone else. Two riders came to grief, but they scrambled to their feet none the worse for their tumble.

'Lorna, Isobel, which of the riders do you think will win this time?' On receiving no response she looked down. Neither Lorna nor Isobel were at her side. She spun and stared around the crowd, they were nowhere in sight. Carefully scanning the crowd gathered within the enclosure she immediately ascertained that the girls were not there. With what she hoped was a relaxed expression she turned to the two little girls who were being held up on the shoulders of the grooms.

'Lottie, Beth, I think the Punch and Judy show is about to begin. Why don't you go along with Nancy and Jo and find us a good place to stand. I shall join you with your sisters directly.'

Dr Moorcroft summed up the situation. 'Off you, go little ones, Miss Shaw and I will follow in a moment. Tommy and Bill remain behind, if you please.'

4

Sarah barely restrained herself from wringing her hands in distress. As soon as the girls had gone she turned to the doctor. 'I know where they will have gone, Isobel mentioned yesterday that she wanted to see the caravans. I fear she has taken Lorna to the Romany camp, I believe they are encamped in the woodland behind this green.'

He nodded. 'Then it's fortunate we have these men to accompany us. In my experience strangers are not welcome.' Taking her shaking hand he pushed it protectively through his arm and squeezed it gently. 'They will come to no harm, Miss Shaw, the gypsies might have a bad name but I have found them respectable people, it's their mode of living that alarms.'

Attempting to look as if she was strolling nonchalantly through the throng,

Sarah constantly looked from side to side hoping to spot the two children. Suddenly she stopped, she was almost sure she saw one of them behind the tent in which the fortune teller sat.

'Over there, I'm sure it was one of the girls. Isobel has green ribbon around her bonnet, Lorna has pink, it's impossible to tell them apart unless they are seated in front of one.'

She removed her hand from his arm and walked briskly towards the booth. Behind it, sobbing quietly, was Lorna. The child threw herself into Sarah's arms mumbling incoherently. 'My love, you are safe now. Here let me wipe your eyes, then you can tell me where Isobel is hiding.'

Through whimpers and gulps the girl was able to explain that her sister had led her into the middle of the fair and then abandoned her. 'I begged her not to leave me, Miss Shaw, but she laughed and said I was a baby and she would go on an adventure on her own.'

'Tell me, sweetheart, where has

Isobel gone? Miss Shaw will take you to watch the Punch and Judy and I shall go and find your naughty sister.'

Lorna pointed in the direction of the woods. Sarah's heart thumped painfully. It was as she feared, she prayed that Dr Moorcroft was not mistaken about the travelling folk. Papa had once told her that village children sometimes disappeared forever when the gypsies were nearby.

He ruffled the child's hair and straightened. 'Don't look so stricken, Miss Shaw, I shall recover your lost sheep and return her to you safe and sound very shortly. Do I have your permission to scold her for her disobedience?'

Sarah nodded. It would do the child no harm to be reprimanded by such a formidable character. Perhaps she would think twice about misbehaving if Dr Moorcroft gave her a stern talking to. 'Please, sir, do hurry. I shall never forgive myself if anything has harmed Isobel. I should not have taken my eyes from them, I was too involved in the races.'

'You have nothing with which to blame yourself, my dear. It was the matter of moments for the girls to slip away; however vigilant you were if Isobel was determined to sneak off she would have done so anyway.'

He smiled, and something most peculiar happened, her toes felt as if they curled up in her walking boots. 'Come along, Lorna, we must join the others. Shall we buy everyone a barley twist to suck whilst we watch the entertainment? I'm sure that Dr Moorcroft will return with Isobel very soon.'

The purchase of confectionery had been all that was needed to take Lorna's mind off her sister's disappearance. When they reached the crowd of children sitting on the grass in front of the Punch and Judy stall she was laughing and chattering as if she had no care in the world. Nancy was watching out for them, the girl raised her eyebrows and Sarah shook her head quickly. No more was necessary.

'See what Miss Shaw has brought us,

Lottie, Beth. Here's a barley sugar for each of you. Has it started yet? Have I missed anything?'

All three girls found themselves a place in front of the booth leaving Sarah to speak to the two anxious maids. 'Miss Isobel went to the gypsy camp. Dr Moorcroft has gone to find her. We are to wait here until he returns.'

A gasp of anticipation rippled through the audience as the tiny striped curtains slowly parted heralding the start of the much awaited show. Nancy and Jo went to sit with the girls leaving her to wander disconsolately around the fringes of the crowd. Dr Moorcroft was head and shoulders taller than most men there, she would be able to see him from some distance away.

It wasn't until the final cheer had died away that she spotted him moving rapidly in her direction. He was holding Isobel in his arms, neither looked happy about this state of affairs.

'Girls, your sister is about to rejoin

us. I intend to send her home with Nancy, she does not deserve to stay for the festivities.' She nodded to the nursery maid. 'Miss Isobel is to go to her room. She is to have no supper and is not to leave her chamber until tomorrow morning.'

'I understand, Miss Shaw. I shall move Lorna's night things in with Miss Charlotte and Miss Elizabeth, it will do Miss Isobel no harm at all to spend the night alone.'

Sarah was impressed by the girl's sensible suggestion. 'Excellent; Tom must drive you back and then return for us. I'm sure that Dr Moorcroft will stay until we depart.'

Isobel was rigid with embarrassment at having been carried like a baby in leading strings across the grass. Dr Moorcroft dumped her unceremoniously. 'She was where we suspected. I have told her how displeased you are, that it would serve her right if you informed her parents.'

'Isobel, I am disappointed in you. You

gave me your word that you would stay at my side and deliberately broke your promise. You are returning at once with Nancy, we shall be remaining here to enjoy ourselves.' She turned her back and smiled happily at the other three children. 'Shall we go and see the fire eaters or would you prefer to look at the stalls and spend some of the money your mama gave me?'

With Nancy holding one elbow and Tommy the other the miscreant was escorted away. Sarah would try not to worry about how she would deal with things on the morrow, today she would concentrate on making sure the others enjoyed themselves.

'Miss Shaw, I suspect that you will have trouble from that one, she is not used to being gainsaid, but I believe in time you might win her round. A week or two away from her mother's overindulgence will be a good start in Isobel's rehabilitation.'

'Where was she? Did she have time to reach the camp?'

'Unfortunately she did, she was surrounded by a group of grubby urchins when we arrived. I believe her interest in these people is at an end.' He scooped up Beth and swung her on to his shoulders. 'Right, let us away to see fire eaters and stilt walkers. I believe that they are on the other side of the Green.'

By the time they returned to Bentley Manor all three of the children were drooping with fatigue. Sarah offered to assist Jo with their bedtime routines.

'Don't you worry, miss, Nancy will have put Miss Isobel to bed long ago, she'll be free to do her chores as usual. It's a real worry, Miss Isobel is becoming wilder as time passes. I fear she may do herself a mischief one of these days.'

Sarah smiled and shook her head sadly. 'I believe it is going to take me longer than I thought to persuade Miss Isobel to conform. I pray that she will listen to me before Sir John decides to send her away to school. That will break

70

the heart of Lady Fenwick for sure.'

Isobel had never spent a night alone in her entire life, it was a harsh punishment but a stand had to be made if things were to be run smoothly in the schoolroom.

Isobel seemed suitably penitent the next day and apologised handsomely for misbehaving. Sarah set her two pages of handwriting as a punishment which was to be done whilst the rest of them were outside enjoying the sunshine. Perhaps the child had learnt her lesson.

On her return to the schoolroom she discovered Isobel collapsed over her desk sobbing. 'My dear, whatever is wrong? Are you feeling unwell?' The girl was too distressed to answer, continuing to weep piteously.

Nancy drew Sarah to one side. 'Sir John came in, word had got to him about Miss Isobel's running off yesterday. He told her she was to be sent away to school in September. I've never seen him so vexed. It will be the end of her, Miss Shaw, and her poor Mama.'

'I shall go down and speak to him directly, ask if he will give her one more chance to show that she can change her behaviour.'

The crying girl pushed herself upright, her face blotched with tears, her nose running; would not such a sight wring the heartstrings of even the most hard-hearted. 'Please, Miss Shaw, I promise I shall never be naughty again. I cannot be sent away, I could not bear it, I should die.'

Sarah gave Isobel her handkerchief and hugged her briefly, relieved that the other girls were in the nursery and had not heard this melodramatic statement. 'I shall do my best, now, go and wash your face and join the others for your lemonade and biscuits.'

Although she searched the down-stairs rooms she could find no sign of Sir John, she was reluctant to speak to the staff, but eventually one of the footmen told her that her employer was out and about on estate business. Dr

Moorcroft stepped out of Lady Fenwick's apartment as she reached that part of the house.

'I am so glad to see you, Isobel is beside herself because Sir John is sending her away to boarding school. Is Lady Fenwick well enough for me to go in and speak to her?'

'Yes, she is desperate for company.' He grinned at her and held the door wide open. 'I believe that you will find this a storm in a tea cup, Miss Shaw.' Then his expression sobered and he drew her to one side. 'All the children are well, I trust?'

'Perfectly, why do you ask?'

'Professional curiosity, think nothing of it. Perhaps when I come another time I could join you and the girls on the promenade around the gardens? I was watching from the window, and Lady Fenwick suggested it herself.'

Sarah's heart skipped a beat at the thought of spending time with the handsome gentlemen, and with the approval of her employer as well. 'I shall look forward to it, sir.' She smiled and slipped past him.

Lady Fenwick was resting on a day bed and greeted her warmly. 'I thought I heard your voice, Miss Shaw. I was expecting you to come down. Is Isobel very distressed?'

'You know that Sir John is sending her away?'

'Sit down, my dear, and I shall explain it all to you.'

Sir John had indeed intended to send his eldest daughter away, but his wife had persuaded him to give the girl another chance. As he would walk over hot coals to please his wife he had reluctantly agreed. But what was abundantly clear, was that if Isobel transgressed again, there would be no reprieve. Lady Fenwick begged Sarah to keep Isobel out of mischief as this was her very last opportunity to prove she was able to conform.

Isobel took her final warning to heart, as each day passed her expression became less pinched, her eyes less wary

and by the Wednesday she was unrecog-
nizable as the unpleasant little girl she'd
met the previous week. Unfortunately
Dr Moorcroft had not yet joined her in
the garden. Betty told her he was no
longer making daily visits as Lady
Fenwick was so much better. It was
almost ten days after their visit to the
fair when Sarah took the children out
to play cricket.

Sarah had taken to visiting Lady
Fenwick whilst the children had their
mid-morning snack to update her
ladyship with the girls' progress. It was
a pleasure to be able to tell her
employer that *all* the girls were doing
well. It had been agreed that the girls
were finally to meet their new brother,
and see their mama, the following day.

When Sarah told them they were
overjoyed. She was surprised that Isobel
did not make more of the news. The girl
was particularly subdued that afternoon, preferring to lounge in the shade
of the large oak tree and not join in the
riotous game of cricket. This was most

unlike her as she was by far the best at striking the ball.

'Nancy, I think that Miss Isobel is poorly. Would you take her in, I think she would be better resting on her bed in the cool, rather them out here in the hot sunshine.'

★   ★   ★

Something disturbed Sarah in the small hours, she was never able to say what it was, but she found herself wide awake. She had been dreaming about Isobel; she would go and check that she was no worse. She had asked to retire before supper saying that she had the headache.

On entering the bed chamber she could see two small shapes under the covers, one was curled up sleeping peacefully, but the other was tossing from side to side as though wrapped in a nightmare. Quickly walking across to offer comfort, Sarah held up her candlestick. It was Isobel, she was not having a nightmare, she was delirious.

She touched the child's cheek, it was burning beneath her fingers. Whatever the little girl had contracted it was not a summer cold, it was something far more serious. Hurrying round to the farther side of the bed she flipped back the covers and lifted the sleeping Lorna out.

Fortunately the little bed, that had been made up for her the night of Isobel's disgrace, was still in the other bed chamber. Without waking the child she placed her between the sheets and then crept out. She must wake Nancy and Jo, one must begin to sponge Isobel with cool water to try and reduce the fever. She would write a note to Dr Moorcroft and the other nursemaid must run downstairs and rouse the housekeeper. This august lady would arrange to send the letter.

Forty-five minutes had dragged by before she heard the firm footsteps of the doctor approaching. Sarah stood aside to let him examine his patient.

She waited, her hands clenched, praying it would not be the news she feared.

He stepped back and turned to face her. 'I'm afraid it is serious, Miss Shaw, I'm certain the child has measles. Her three sisters will be infected too, we cannot risk the illness reaching the new arrival. You must be quarantined away from here.' He carefully washed his hands and dried them. 'I feared as much when I received your note. There have been several cases already in the village, and it would seem children in the Romany encampment were the carriers. This is where Isobel must have contracted it.'

'But where can we go? Is there anywhere suitable on the estate? Isobel is too sick to take far.'

'You must come to my house, I have dozens of empty bedrooms and more than enough staff to cope with the demands of nursing sickly children. Get your maid to pack your necessities, I shall organise the rest.'

Without asking if Sarah was agreeable, he strode out, presumably to speak to Sir John and arrange for carriages to be harnessed. Heaven knows what her employer would think of being dragged from his bed at this time of the night. She thanked God that Isobel had succumbed to this disease *before* visiting her baby brother.

There was no other option, but there was one thing Dr Moorcroft had *not* considered when he issued his instructions. What would the neighbourhood think about an unmarried woman living unchaperoned in a bachelor establishment? Would her reputation be in tatters, or was a mere governess too insignificant to count?

An hour after Dr Moorcroft had left her Sarah was sitting in a luxurious carriage with Isobel's head resting on her lap. Betty accompanied her, the other three girls were travelling in a separate vehicle with Nancy and Jo. Her maid was balancing a jug of cold water in her lap; Sarah bathed the child's burning face with a wet cloth and then returned it to be refreshed. There was nothing else she could do until they reached their destination.

She could scarcely credit that she was removing from Bentley Manor in this unorthodox way. It could well be several weeks before she was able to return with her charges, the incubation period for measles could be as long as two weeks. It would be unwise to leave quarantine until Dr Moorcroft was satisfied none of them could bring the contagion with them.

Although this was an ailment children suffered from, occasionally adults succumbed as well. She had not had time to enquire if the nursery maids were immune. 'Betty, do you recall if you had measles as a child?'

'I had several fevers, but I don't rightly know if any of them were because of the measles. It was good of the doctor to take us in. Mind you, Miss Shaw, it's a huge house he has and only himself and his mother living there. He's a widower, you know, he moved here a few years back after his wife died. Reckon he . . . '

'That's enough, Betty, we should not be discussing Dr Moorcroft's private life. It is none of our business.' Sarah squeezed out the cloth and continued with her ministrations. It was a relief that she would not be unchaperoned, when she next wrote to Mama she would not have to prevaricate about the circumstances of the move to Bentley village. Her eyes pricked and she swallowed the lump in her throat. She hated to think of her dearest mother being obliged to live as an unpaid companion to an elderly relative; but when her father had passed away his stipend had gone with him.

The new rector of the parish had arrived with his young family and both she and her mother were forced to find alternative arrangements. Sarah had become a governess, her mother had gone to live with a distant cousin. It was her dream that one day they would be reunited in their own home.

The carriage slowed and in the moonlight she saw an imposing gatepost, almost immediately they were stationary. The door was snatched open.

'Miss Shaw, allow me to take the child, I have a chamber prepared. The sooner we get her settled the better. The next forty eight hours will prove crucial to the outcome of this.'

Leaving Betty to tip out the remainder of the water, Sarah followed him up the steps and into a large vestibule. She scarcely had time to take in her surroundings as he bounded up the stairs and she was obliged to hurry after him. A small army of male servants were already unloading the luggage. No doubt this would be dealt with by the chambermaids. It was a miracle of organisation that the doctor had marshalled his staff in the middle of the night in this way.

'I have opened the east wing for your use. I'm afraid you and the girls must remain up here until I am certain they are clear of infection.'

He shouldered his way through a half open door and carried Isobel through a commodious parlour and into the bed chamber. She watched him place the girl tenderly in the waiting bed. All the windows were wide open, but the drapes were drawn making the room cool and dark. There were a further three small beds in the room. He was obviously anticipating the other girls catching the disease.

'I shall continue to bathe her with cold water unless you have any other instructions for me.'

'No, I do not. You seem a sensible young woman, I shall leave the child's care to you for the moment. I am going to examine the other three, it's quite possible they will succumb before the day is out.'

'I see that everything is ready if they do. Is there alternative accommodation for the children?'

He yawned and rubbed his eyes,

grinning apologetically. 'I beg your pardon, Miss Shaw. I had just returned from another call when your missive arrived. I have yet to seek my bed.'

'Then I shall not detain you, Dr Moorcroft. I shall send word to you if Isobel's condition worsens.'

5

Adam was happy to discover the other three girls had no fever, no sign of a runny nose or dry cough, at least for the moment. He could scarcely keep his eyes open, whereas a few years ago he could have stayed up for two days without being fatigued. He smiled ruefully, he considered himself in his prime at three and thirty, but his body was telling him otherwise. He would retire, hopefully he would get a few hours sleep before he was called to the sick room, or anywhere else.

His mother would be delighted to have visitors even if they were to be constrained in the east wing for the moment. Although she had made several friends in the neighbourhood, she found the quiet of the countryside a sore trial after having spent most of her life in the city.

It hardly seemed worth undressing, the dawn chorus had already started, it would be full light soon. He stretched out on top of the comforter, having first pulled off his boots. He closed his eyes and let his mind drift over the events of that fateful day; when he'd seen Miss Shaw and her entourage arrived his first instinct had been to walk the other way. But something had impelled him to travel in her direction — she was the antithesis of everything he admired in a young lady.

Slowly he reviewed her attributes; she was overly tall and then, her hair was an indeterminate brown colour, she had far too much to say for herself and disliked horses. His lips curved, from this list one would think she was an antidote. Nothing of the sort; she was kind and intelligent, certainly coura-geous and not afraid of hard work, but what attracted him were her eyes. As he drifted into sleep his head filled with the image of sea green eyes deep enough to drown in.

The next morning he rolled from his bed and startled his manservant who was preparing the equipment to shave him. 'Edwards, I require clean linen; I shall shave myself this morning, it will wake me up.'

Adam was relieved there had been no summons to the east wing, this must mean Isobel was no worse. He was sharp set, he would break his fast and then seek out his mother and tell her about the unexpected arrivals. She would be wondering what was going on in the normally too quiet house.

When he strode into the breakfast parlour he was surprised to find her already there.

'My dear, you look quite exhausted. I had thought when we removed here to the country I would see more of you, not less.' His mother pointed to the chair next to hers and dutifully he folded himself on to it. The footman was well aware what he liked to eat in the morning, would bring over his heaped plate. The coffee jug already on the table.

'I like to keep occupied, Mama, it gives me less time to dwell on the past. It is likely to be even busier in the future. No doubt you have heard that I have made the east wing into a quarantine ward; Sir John's oldest girl has contracted measles, she is being nursed up there by her governess. The other three girls are well at the moment, and have their own nurse-maids to take care of them.'

'Good heavens! I can see why you did so, my dear, you cannot risk the health of the new baby. Celia Fenwick told me you advised her against this last pregnancy, so this much longed for son will be the last child she bears.'

'Exactly so, unless she wishes to leave her children motherless, she will avoid further childbearing.' He smiled at his mother, she understood his need to unburden himself sometimes and respected the confidentiality of these exchanges.

'Miss Shaw, the governess, is she to join us for dinner tonight?'

'No, she cannot leave her charges. Don't pucker up, Mama, she is here to do a job, not to socialise.'

'Of course she is, but I hope I will have an opportunity to meet her before she leaves. I assume she is of a more robust personality than the last two specimens Celia employed.'

He chuckled. 'Miss Shaw is as different to them as chalk is to cheese. I must admit that I did not take to her at first, but on further acquaintance I'm finding her more to my liking.'

'I should think you did not, my dear, after she caused you to go headfirst into a hedge that night. Is she a comely young woman?'

This enquiry was not as innocent as it sounded, his mama was constantly throwing out hints that it was high time he looked for another wife. Martha had been dead for more than five years; he rarely saw her face now, but sometimes he could still hear her soft Irish brogue in his head as he was falling asleep.

'She has mouse brown hair, is above average height and thin as a rail. However she has a lively intelligence and is excellent with her charges.' He refrained from mentioning her amazing eyes.

'Those girls are dreadfully spoilt, Celia should have known better. It's small wonder that governesses only remain in that establishment for a short time. Do you think Miss Shaw will do any better?'

'I do, she's a most unusual young lady. I don't believe I told you what happened in the schoolroom that first day?' His mother was impressed when she heard of Miss Shaw's composure and decreed she would go up later and introduce herself. 'You cannot, Mama, the east wing is an isolation ward at the moment.'

'Adam, I am well aware that measles is highly infectious, but surely it only passes from those that already have the illness? Presumably Miss Shaw is not so afflicted and neither am I. I shall invite her to come down and take coffee with me, we have ample staff to watch the girls in her absence.'

He admitted defeat. He would like to see what his mother thought of the girl who was occupying far too much of his thoughts.

Sarah looked up as the bedroom door opened. It had been a long night, but she was sure Isobel was improving. Although she was coughing dreadfully her fever was lower. Her face was now liberally sprinkled with the tell-tale red marks, until the rash fully developed the girl would still be in danger of complications. 'Betty, I'm glad to see you. Can I leave you to watch our patient whilst I refresh myself and check on the other girls.'

'I've spoken to Nancy, miss, all three are full of beans. Why don't you go and get some sleep, miss, I promise to rouse you if there is any need.'

'I should dearly like to do that, but I have no idea in which chamber I am situated.'

'You have the room directly opposite this one, I have laid out your night things and there's hot water in the dressing room. I've left you chocolate and sweet morning rolls, I expect you're starving.'

Food was exactly what she needed, that and a few hours sleep. Yawning hugely she left her capable maid to watch over the sleeping child and stepped into the corridor coming face-to-face with her host.

'Good morning, Miss Shaw, I take it our patient is doing well.'

Quickly swallowing her yawn Sarah forced her lips to smile, she was well aware that her dress was sadly crumpled and her face etched with fatigue. It should not matter, but for some reason it did. 'Isobel's fever is somewhat reduced, the rash is appearing and she's sleeping. I would not have agreed to leave her otherwise. Also the other girls remain unaffected for the moment. I am returning to my chamber in order to write a letter to Sir John and

Lady Fenwick telling them the crisis for Isobel is over.'

He raised a hand as if to take her arm and then thought better of it. 'I shall inform both parents when I visit this morning. I have several other calls to make, I doubt I shall be around until later this afternoon, there have been several cases of measles in the village.' He smiled own at her and she couldn't help responding. 'On a lighter note, my mother wishes to meet you. When you are rested, perhaps you would consider going down and introducing yourself?'

Disconcerted by his invitation, her cheeks coloured. 'Thank you, Dr Moorcroft, if I am able to snatch a half an hour, I would love to go down and meet Mrs Moorcroft. Pray excuse me, I have not eaten since yesterday morning and there is a tray waiting in my parlour.'

He nodded, she noticed that his eyes crinkled endearingly at the corners when he was smiling. She whisked into her room hoping he hadn't been aware that she was staring at him. She had never felt the slightest interest in a gentleman before. She had been introduced to several hopeful young men whilst her father had been alive, but none of them had made her heart beat faster the way *this* one did.

Not bothering to undress completely she stretched out on the bed feeling pleasantly full after her repast. She would rest for a couple of hours and then taken the children for a walk in the gardens; as long as they met no one else that should be perfectly safe. She sighed, she supposed she'd better speak to Dr Moorcroft before the girls left the east wing.

Much refreshed after her rest, Sarah put her green muslin gown back on, straightened her hair and was ready to return to her duties. The sound of childish laughter below her window made her hurry over and look out. To her astonishment her host was outside playing cricket with the girls, Nancy and Jo were joining in enthusiastically.

Surely he was supposed to be out on calls this morning?

Smiling at their antics she waved, immediately he waved back and Lorna beckoned her. She would join them, but on the way it would be polite to stop and speak to Mrs Moorcroft. A parlour maid directed her to the drawing-room, but did not offer to announce her or hold the doors open. It was a relief to discover they did not stand on ceremony here, unlike Bentley Manor.

She hesitated outside the door, then taking a deep breath she knocked on the door. Immediately she was bid enter and immediately found herself face-to-face with a small, plump woman with fading brown hair.

'Miss Shaw, do come in, I have been anticipating your arrival this past hour. Adam said you would call in after you had rested. He tells me your little patient is doing well, has taken some broth, and is no longer in any danger.'

Sarah curtsied politely. 'I cannot tell you how grateful I am that you were able to accommodate us all at such short notice. Dr Moorcroft has said we must remain here for a full two weeks after the last symptom of the measles has gone. So far no one else has shown signs of the disease, I'm praying that it might be only Isobel who has caught it.'

'It's too soon to say that the other little girls have been spared, but if none of them develop any symptoms within two weeks, then I think you can safely say they are not going to catch it. Won't you sit with me for a while, Miss Shaw, tell me a little about yourself.'

'If you will excuse me on this occasion, ma'am, I'm on my way to play cricket in the garden with the children.'

Mrs Moorcroft rustled to her feet, her burgundy silk gown swirling about her ankles. 'Then if you are not needed in the sickroom, please join us for dinner. We keep country hours . . . ' she laughed. 'Indeed, I should rephrase that. Dinner is supposed to be eaten at five o'clock, however it is frequently far later than that because Adam is out visiting a patient somewhere. Hopefully tonight he will not be called away.'

'I should be delighted to join you, if I can. However, I do not have an evening gown. Do you dress for dinner?'

'Good heavens, no, my dear. Adam dislikes formality of any sort; come as you are. That is a delightful gown, you should always wear green as it complements your eyes.'

★ ★ ★

Outside she was greeted with hugs and kisses from her charges and a charming smile from her host. It was a pleasure to see a gentleman so at ease with children, she couldn't imagine why she had ever thought him disagreeable. Eventually it was agreed the game was over and Nancy and Jo returned the girls to their temporary nursery leaving Sarah to stroll back with Dr Moorcroft.

'I can't remember when I've enjoyed myself so much, Miss Shaw. I have little leisure time; as a rule I prefer to keep busy.'

'I had been intending to ask you if it was permissible to bring Lottie, Beth and Lorna into the gardens. I'm delighted that you consider it safe for them to be outside like this.'

'As long as they remain on this side of the house, there's little danger of them meeting any other children. I must warn you, Miss Shaw, there have been two deaths already from this epidemic. Both children were from the gypsy encampment, I'm hoping they will be the only ones.'

She shuddered and sent up a quick prayer to the Almighty for the souls of the departed little ones. 'How long before we know if the others have contracted the disease?'

'The incubation period is ten to twelve days, although sometimes when the strain is particularly virulent it can appear much sooner. I have had a most enjoyable hour, but now I must return to my duties. No doubt we will meet again tomorrow.'

'Mrs Moorcroft has invited me to dine with you, so we might well meet sooner than that.'

One finely arched eyebrow raised, something flashed across his eyes and then he was smiling blandly. 'In which case, Miss Shaw, I had better make an effort to be on time.' He nodded, waved a nonchalant hand and strode off in the direction of the stables. Sarah was left unsure whether he was displeased or not by her disclosure.

She spent the remainder of the day with Isobel whose fever had risen again, although this time she was not delirious. It was obvious she was not going to be able to go down for dinner, she would send her regrets with a footman. She was disappointed to miss this opportunity to get to know both the doctor and his delightful mother.

'Nancy, you must go and eat, then retire early. I shall stay with Isobel until you come to relieve me. She is far too poorly to be left, even for a moment.'

⋆　⋆　⋆

For the next few days Sarah was fully occupied nursing Isobel, then no sooner was this patient on the way to recovery than one by one the other girls succumbed. Lorna was fortunate, within three days she was well enough to return to the bedroom allocated to her and Isobel. Lessons had been suspended until everyone was well, the only good news was that Lady Fenwick was fully recovered and now allowed to leave her chambers and the new baby was in perfect health.

Almost two weeks after her arrival at The Rookery, she was sitting in the fading light reading her Gothic novel she had found in the library, it was her intention to sit up all night in the sickroom. Although Beth was making a good recovery her sister had taken a turn for the worse. Her fever had risen steadily all day, Jo was sitting at the bedside sponging the little girl with cold water.

'Miss Shaw, come quick, Miss Lottie sounds mighty strange.'

Sarah immediately dropped her book and hurried over. 'You are quite correct, her breathing is erratic. Go at once to the drawing-room and fetch Dr Moorcroft.'

Whilst she waited she dropped to her knees beside the bed and asked God to intervene. The doctor was beside her in minutes. She straightened and stood to one side to let him examine the patient.

'I'm glad that you sent for me, but I fear there's little I can do. The illness has affected her lungs, you must prepare yourself for the worst.'

Beth, who was in one of the little beds on the far side of the room, stirred in her sleep. 'Shall I move Beth? I should not like her to be in the room if anything . . . ' She could not continue, her throat was clogged with tears.

'A good idea. Let me carry her through, she can return to the chamber she was sharing with Charlotte.' He nodded at Jo. 'Come with me, you must take care of this little one now.'

Sarah sat on a footstool beside Lottie, the child's skin was hot and dry, her breathing ever more laboured. In the flickering light of the candles she detected a change in the child's appearance; her complexion was pale, dark circles around her eyes. She squeezed out the water from the cloth she was holding and continued in her attempt to lower the fever.

A hand dropped to her shoulder. 'I should desist, my dear, it will do no good. There's little either of us can do but sit and offer what comfort we can.' His voice was thick with tears, he was as moved as she by the plight of the child.

'Do we need to send to Bentley Manor? Should not her parents be here with her?'

'No, Lottie . . . I mean . . . I don't believe we have sufficient time to send word.'

Sarah scrambled to her feet and tenderly lifted the little girl into her arms then leant back against the wall. At least she could hold Lottie, she didn't want her to be frightened. Sarah prayed that a miracle might happen, that the child would open her eyes and smile at them.

The bed dipped as he joined her on the other side. He slid one arm behind her, gathering her and the dying child within his embrace. Her tears dripped unheeded down her cheeks, she murmured loving words and Lottie's fingers closed around hers for a second, and then slackened.

The room was hideously silent, the painful breathing stopped for ever.

6

Sarah turned instinctively to the comfort of Dr Moorcroft's arms. She rested her face against his shoulder unable to contain her sobs; it was so unfair, Charlotte had all her life ahead of her, had been taken at the tender age of seven.

'My dear, you must leave her now. There are things that have to be done, and I must go and give the dreadful news to her parents.' Gently he mopped Sarah's face with his own handkerchief and then lifted her from the bed.

'Do I have to tell her sisters? They will be devastated, especially Isobel.'

'I think it's better to keep the news to ourselves for the moment, my dear, I'm sure that Sir John will wish to break it himself. It's fortunate that they're all fast asleep, they need know nothing until the morning.'

Sarah needed his arm around her waist in order to remain on her feet. She had been there at the death of her father, but to see a child breath her last was far worse. Lottie looked as though she was asleep, her eyes were closed, she looked peaceful. It was small comfort to know the little girl was in a better place for she would be sorely missed by her family and herself.

'Will the shock of this tragedy cause problems for Lady Fenwick?'

'I hope not; her heart condition does not appear to be adversely affected by stress. It is only the strain of childbirth that appears to cause difficulty.'

'I must wash my face and then take a turn in the garden to recover my composure.'

* * *

Adam wanted to gather her back in his arms, she looked so sad. 'Why don't you come with me to Bentley Manor? It would be better if you broke the news to Lady Fenwick, I shall speak to Sir John.'

Her remarkable eyes widened, he thought she was going to refuse, and he wouldn't have blamed her. 'I will come if you believe it will help. I cannot think of anything worse than hearing of the death of a beloved child. I know that children die every day, but I didn't know any of those. Lottie was such a sweet girl.' Her voice trembled, her fists clenched and she swallowed several times before being able to continue. 'I shall be ready to leave in ten minutes. Will that be long enough for you to make your arrangements?'

As she was speaking he gradually led her from the room. 'I shall call for you when the carriage is outside, you may tell your abigail, but she must keep the information to herself. It is still another hour before full dark, quite long enough to travel the two miles to Bentley Manor.'

'If Nancy and Jo are not to be told, there will be no one to sit with Lottie.

She should not be alone, even though she is . . . though she is . . . ' Unable to continue she held his sodden handkerchief to her mouth as if trying to keep back her sobs and rushed into her own chamber.

He must speak to the housekeeper, Mrs Taylor, she knew what was required at this difficult time. She had been with the family since he was a boy, had dealt with such tragedies on more than one occasion. He would inform his mother, she would be waiting most anxiously downstairs. Miss Shaw would be better for some sympathetic female company.

He wasn't sure why he was so concerned for the welfare of a young woman he'd only met a few weeks ago; she wasn't particularly pretty. Apart from her eyes, that is — but he was beginning to think that his feelings towards her weren't strictly professional. He was unsure if he was ready to declare himself, and today was certainly not an appropriate time to be talking of romantic matters.

His mother was standing quietly in the centre of the room, her expression grave. 'There's no need to explain, my boy, I knew at once from your expression that it was the worst possible news.'

'Miss Shaw has taken it very badly, do you think you could go up and speak to her? I have asked her to come with me to break the news to Lady Fenwick, I cannot think what possessed me to do such a thing. It will be too harrowing for her, if you can keep her occupied I shall slip away on my own. Unfortunately I have had to be the bearer of bad tidings many times over the past few years.'

'I shall go upstairs at once. Do you wish me to speak to Mrs Taylor?'

He shook his head. 'I shall do it, thank you, Mama.' He rubbed his eyes, it never got any easier, every time he lost a patient he was deeply upset. Medical men were supposed to remain aloof from the people they treated, but he found that impossible. 'Don't wait up for me, I have no idea how long I shall be. If you can persuade Miss Shaw to come downstairs, she will be better away from what must be done in the bed chamber adjacent to hers.'

* * *

Sarah looked up tiredly as Betty ushered Mrs Moorcroft into the bed chamber. 'My dear girl, you must not distress yourself. Elizabeth and the twins will need you to be strong, if you give way to your grief how are they to cope?'

'Madam, you're right to chide me. I have been sitting here crying when I should have been getting ready to go out.'

'Adam has decided to go on his own, he apologises for having asked you, it's not your task to break bad news. Why don't you come downstairs to the drawing-room, I shall order the tea tray to be brought through. A hot drink will do us both good.'

The last thing Sarah wanted was to sip tea in the drawing room, but she could hardly refuse such a kind invitation. With a clean handkerchief held firmly in one hand she followed her hostess through the house and into the grand room. Mrs Moorcroft had paused to speak briefly to a footman, no doubt that the tray would arrive imminently.

'I have been wondering how I am to arrange to the children's mourning clothes. I have a black dress that I wore when my father died, it is somewhat dated but will be perfectly adequate. But the children?'

'It's not your concern, my dear, Lady Fenwick will decide if she wishes her daughters to wear black. It's not obligatory you know. Personally I think children should be exempt from the custom, to put on the same black gown day after day for months cannot possibly allow them to move on with their lives. It would be a constant reminder of their loss.'

Sarah collapsed on to the nearest chair; her limbs seemed to have little strength in them at the moment, it was as if she was weighed down by something heavy she could not see. It had not been this way when Papa had died.

'But should I wear black?'

'Leave such decisions to your employers, my dear, after all you have only been at Bentley Manor for a few weeks. You could not possibly be expected to anticipate their wishes after such a short time.'

The tea tray appeared and Mrs Moorcroft busied herself with the urn. Sarah closed her eyes. Would they all return home sooner because of this tragedy? Only Beth was unwell, and she would be fully recovered in a day or two.

'Here, my dear, sit up and drink this. You will feel a lot better if you do.'

A delicate porcelain cup and saucer was placed in her trembling fingers, it took all her concentration not to drop it. Slowly she raised the cup and sipped the hot liquid, she almost spat it out again. It had been heavily sugared, something she could not abide. Somehow she swallowed the mouthful and put the drink down. Her distaste must have been written on her face.

'I know, my dear, but Adam is always telling me that a hot, sweet drink is good for shock.'

'If I drink it, ma'am, I shall cast up my accounts. A most dreadful thought has occurred to me, shall Sir John blame Isobel for his daughter's death?'

'It's a possibility, it would be a great shame if he does. The poor child will have enough of a burden to bear without being sent away to a seminary.'

The rattle of the carriage leaving from the turning circle in front of the house meant that the doctor was on his way to break the news. Sarah decided she would wait up until he returned, she couldn't sleep anyway, her grief was too raw.

'Mrs Moorcroft, if you will excuse me, I thank you for your kindness but I'm going to take a walk in the garden before it becomes too dark. It will clear my head.'

'Why don't you walk down to the church? It's no more than a mile from here, and the door is always open.'

* * *

Within half an hour Sarah and Betty were walking down the lane. The sudden cracking of twigs in the hedgerow on the far side startled them both. Betty clutched her arm. 'Miss Shaw, did you hear that?'

'I did, I'm sure it's no more than a night creature. A fox perhaps hunting rabbits in the ditch. We have our lantern, there are dwellings on either side of the lane, I'm sure there's nothing to be bothered about.'

After spending a considerable time in the church in silent prayer Sarah led the way back outside. She was glad she had the forethought to bring a lantern, there was no moon tonight and it was pitch dark outside. She could not help thinking about the strange noise in the hedge, she was certain it had been no animal, but a human lurking there.

In the feeble light she set off briskly, her maid almost running at her side. What had seemed like a friendly place in daylight was now fraught with danger, every snap and rustle made her jerk. Her nervousness was shared by her companion, neither mentioned their fear, but she knew Betty was thinking about the noise. They would be passing the very place at any moment, it was just around the bend.

Should she march past in the centre of the lane as if oblivious, or slink quietly with their lantern hidden? The decision was taken from her hands as two rough figures loomed in front of them, one holding a cudgel, the other a knife.

★ ★ ★

Adam was glad to escape from Bentley Manor. He didn't want to return in the carriage, he needed to stretch his legs. He could not recall a more harrowing interview than the one he'd just had with Sir John. Initially the news had been taken with stoicism, the details had been demanded and given. Miss Shaw and the children were not to go into mourning, but they were to remain at The Rookery until after the funeral.

Sir John had asked him to stay whilst he broke the news to Lady Fenwick and Adam had paced the drawing-room awaiting the gentleman's return. Twenty minutes had gone by before heavy footsteps approached the door. He turned and waited, his eyes had narrowed at what he saw. Could this be the same person who had left him a while ago? He would never forget what was spoken then.

'I have come to a decision, Moorcroft, Isobel will not reside under this roof again. My beloved Lottie would still be alive today if it hadn't been for that girl's disobedience. Arrangements will be made in the morning, when Miss Shaw returns with Elizabeth and Lorna, Isobel will be collected and taken to a suitable school.'

Nothing Adam had said had been able to dissuade him from his harsh decision. Sir John could not accept that separating the three girls at such a time would aggravate their suffering. Even explaining to him that his wife's grief would be doubled to lose two daughters instead of one had done no good. He could only pray that as his grief lessened Sir John would reconsider. It would do no good to tell Miss Shaw, or the girls, of this decision at the moment.

He told his coachman to take the carriage home, he refused the offer of a lantern on a pole taken from the front of the carriage. His night vision was excellent; he preferred to walk in the dark, it suited his mood at the moment.

He strode down the lane trying to make sense of what had happened. Tonight the glorious song of the nightingales did nothing to improve his humour. He was wrenched from his sound reverie by a woman's scream. He raced in the direction of the cry, he had recognized the lady in distress. It was Sarah, she was in danger.

★　★　★

'Run, Betty, fetch help from the house we just passed.' It was she the men wanted, a maid servant did not carry a reticule full of money. They must have seen them passing and lain in wait.

It was impossible to see the faces of her attackers, in her fright Betty had dropped the lantern. It would be better to relinquish her bag without protest. 'I have little money, but what I have you may take.' She held it out, the larger of the two snatched it from a hand.

'We'll 'ave yer necklace and yer watch, 'and them over sharpish.' The larger of the two snarled.

They could not have her cross and chain, it had been a confirmation present from her father. She backed away, but they rushed at her and she could not hold back her scream.

Despite the strong arms holding her she lashed out with her booted feet, several times her kicks connected with their shins and they swore viciously. A filthy hand grabbed her cross and tore it from her neck. She stumbled to her knees gasping for breath. She was aware that another man had arrived and floored the footpad who had snatched her necklace. Sinking to the dirt she buried her head in her hands, it was too much after all that had happened tonight.

Suddenly she was cradled in familiar arms. 'You are safe now, my love, the men have run off. I have recovered your chain. Did they hurt you when they removed it?'

For a moment she rested in his embrace waiting for her breathing to steady. 'I am perfectly well now, sir, but if it had not been for your timely intervention I should have lost the most precious item I own.'

He seemed reluctant to release her, was stroking her shoulders and murmuring words of encouragement. The sound of voices approaching from behind made her push him away.

'Someone's coming to my rescue. Could you help me to my feet, please? I do not wish to alarm anyone by being on the ground when they arrive. Betty must have roused the nearest household.'

Lanterns bobbed as several gentlemen hurried towards them. She had no idea who was coming, but her rescuer greeted them by name. 'Mr Oxford, thank you for coming so promptly. Miss Shaw is comparatively unharmed, I was able to discourage them and the vagabonds ran off.'

For an unaccountable reason the figures approaching were becoming blurred, their voices sounded distant.

Sarah swayed and then blackness overwhelmed her.

★ ★ ★

Adam saw her sway and swept her up into his arms. 'The shock has been too much for her, I must get her back where I can take care of her.' Her maid servant was hovering anxiously, her face tear streaked and pale. Thankfully he remembered the woman's name.

'Betty, are you well enough to return to The Rookery? There are several stout men here who can assist you if you wish.'

'No, sir, I can manage. It can't be far to your home from here.'

'Very well, Miss Shaw will require your assistance when we get back.' He turned to his neighbour and the three male servants he had brought with him. 'Sir, I cannot think why those men should wish to attack anyone in this way. Do you think you could call in to speak to me tomorrow morning?'

It was agreed they would meet to discuss this extraordinary event the next day, the men conversed quietly amongst themselves, he could not think about the cause, his concern was for the young woman still in a deep swoon in his arms. He was almost running by the time he reached his own front door.

Betty had gone ahead and his mother was waiting in the doorway to greet them. 'How dreadful, Adam, and tonight of all nights. I have had brandy sent upstairs and tea with no sugar.'

He carried his precious burden to her chamber and placed her gently on the bed. Her pulse was steady, her breathing deeper than he'd expected. He smiled and stepped away. 'I shall leave Miss Shaw to your expert care, Betty, she's in a deep restorative slumber. When you have completed your duties here you must retire. You will be needed first thing tomorrow.'

His heart was light as he left the room. This attack had clarified matters, he understood his feelings now. He was irrevocably in love with Miss Shaw . . . no, she would be Sarah in his heart from now. He could not speak to her at the moment, it would be inappropriate, but before she returned to Bentley Manor he would declare himself.

However, he would tell Mother his good news. They both needed something to cheer them up on this tragic night. Tomorrow was soon enough to puzzle out why Sarah had been targeted in this way. Despite the sadness, something happy had come out of the tragedy. It was true what the old adage said, even the darkest cloud had a silver lining.

7

Sarah opened her eyes to glorious sunshine, for a brief second she felt her heart lift as she recalled that Dr Moorcroft had referred to her as *his love*. In future, dare she think of him by his given name, Adam? Then her happiness fled and reality rushed in to replace it. Sir John would be coming this morning to tell the others, she must be prepared, put her own feelings to one side. Beth, who had been closest in age, would surely feel the loss most strongly. Isobel and Lorna had each other for comfort, had always shared a bed.

There was only one answer, she must move in with Beth — at least for the present. It was too much to expect her to sleep alone. She pushed herself upright, considering the circumstances she felt remarkably refreshed. 'Betty, are you there?'

There was a rustle of skirts to the left of the bed and her abigail appeared. 'I wasn't sure what to put out for you, miss, it should be something black, but that isn't possible until the master has spoken to the girls.'

'It doesn't matter. I shall wear my normal attire; did I hear the sound of a bath being prepared next door?'

'You did, Miss Shaw. I thought you would like a nice hot dip after your nasty experience last night. Mr Oxford says that gypsies are to blame for all the pilfering and damage done in the neighbourhood. He is convinced it was men from that camp.'

Sarah frowned. 'I have little experience of such people, but I have never heard that they attack defenceless women. I think it far more likely to have been a couple of poachers, vagrants who thought they had an opportunity.'

She had little appetite and ate nothing from her breakfast tray. It was her duty to be with the children, but knew that to be impossible until Sir John had visited. There was the sound of childish laughter and the patter of feet in the corridor outside her chamber. Good, Nancy and Jo were taking the girls out to play in the garden. Let them enjoy the sunshine whilst they could.

Once she could see them she hurried from her rooms and down to knock on the drawing-room door. Firm footsteps approached and it was opened.

'Sweetheart, I was about to come up and see you. You look much better this morning.'

'I thank you, sir, for your timely intervention last night. I am fully recovered, but wished to discover when Sir John is expected. I cannot be with the children until they know the truth.'

He took her hands in his and gently drew here into the room closing the door quietly behind them. Immediately his mother arrived at her side and embraced her fondly. 'My dear, come and sit down. I shall order coffee;

perhaps you might eat a little something?'

Sarah sat where directed, she had not the energy to refuse refreshments. The parlourmaid arrived with the tray, there were only two cups upon it. Adam . . . Dr Moorcroft . . . must be going on his rounds.

To her surprise Mrs Moorcroft fluttered to the door. 'I have errands to run, please forgive me but I must leave you alone.' The door was opened and her hostess gone before either of them could protest at the impropriety.

'Don't look so perturbed, my dear, I asked Mama to leave us. There is something most particular I wish to say to you.'

Sarah was on her feet and backing away towards the window before he had finished his speech. She did not want his proposal, although she was certain that she loved him, now was not the time to be discussing matters of the heart. He followed her until she was trapped.

'I know today is not the perfect day for me to declare myself, but, my love, I think it will be much easier to bear the next few days if we can console each other.' Gently he stretched out and captured her trembling fingers. 'Sarah, will you do me the inestimable honour of agreeing to be my wife? I know we cannot think about a future together at the moment, but we can become betrothed, it will give me the right to take care of you.'

His dear face was sincere, his expression anxious, how could she refuse him? 'As long as you realise it might be a considerable while until I am free of my responsibilities, then I am happy to accept your offer.'

In one stride he was next to her, his arms encircled her waist and he drew her close. She could feel his heart pounding, knew he was as moved as she. She tilted her head in order to see his face, there were tears in his eyes and she reached up to brush them away.

'I love you, Sarah Shaw, I will make

you the happiest of brides when the time *is* right. Beth, Lorna, and especially Isobel, will need your loving support over the next few weeks. But I am hoping by the autumn you will be able to resign your position and take up a new one, as my wife.'

'And I love you; I promise as soon as I am able, I will come to you.' Her hands clutched his waistcoat in excitement. 'Would you consider allowing my mother to live with us? She . . . '

Slowly he lowered his head until his mouth was hovering over hers. 'Of course she can; Mama will be delighted to have a companion of her own age.' Then his lips closed over hers in a kiss of such sweetness, such love, that her knees almost gave way.

The crunch of carriage wheels in the gravel outside jolted them apart. It was Sir John come to break the dreadful news to his remaining daughters. 'Shall I go out and collect the children or will you send a servant?'

'I shall go out myself and then

accompany them upstairs. Wait for me there, my love. It's going to be a harrowing business, I wish I had been able to dissuade Sir John from this path.'

The chamber the girls were using as their playroom was a light, spacious room. She was tempted to draw the shutters, block out some of the sunshine, make it more appropriate to the situation. It was Isobel she was most concerned about, the little girl would be devastated to discover she was not to return home with the others, but be sent away to school as punishment for her part in the tragedy. Surely it was enough to know the illness had been brought into the nursery by her?

It took far longer for them to return, only Isobel was fully recovered from the measles and there were a deal of stairs to climb. When they entered the two nursery maids looked enquiringly in her direction. Sarah shook her head and gestured that they should retreat to the dressing room. Adam had carried Beth from the garden and gently placed her on the boards.

Lorna rushed over. 'Miss Shaw, we have missed you. Where have you been all day?' Isobel smiled and nodded her agreement.

'Did we hear a carriage? Has Mama come to visit now that we're all so much better?'

It was Beth who asked the question Sarah had been dreading. 'Where is Lottie? Is she better too?'

Adam shook his head slightly. 'Your papa is here. Ah! I can hear him approaching.'

Immediately the children shrank back, Beth attempting to bury herself in Sarah's skirts, Isobel and Lorna stood behind her. This was not a good start. It was the first intimation she'd had that the girls were in fear of their father — she wished now that the news had been broken by herself. Too late to repine. Sir John was at the door.

He was in full mourning, Isobel's piteous cry wrung her heart. All three must believe it was their beloved mother who had passed away. Sir John remained at the door. He cleared his throat, it was then that she saw his knuckles were white. He was not as composed as she had thought.

'Elizabeth, Lorna, Isobel, I have grievous information for you. Charlotte . . . Lottie . . . died last night.' His harsh words hung in the air. He shifted from one foot to the other. 'The blame for this tragedy is on your shoulders, Isobel. You were given due warning about your behaviour, I do not wish you to return to Bentley manor. You will be going to school when your sisters return.'

This dreadful announcement produced dramatic reactions from all three children. Beth cast up her accounts, Lorna collapsed in a heap sobbing loudly and Isobel, as white as a sheet, fled from the room without a word. By the time Beth and Lorna had been dealt with Sir John had gone. No word of comfort had been offered, Sarah was deeply shocked by his callous behaviour.

'Adam, could you go and find Isobel? I cannot leave Beth and Lorna when they are so distressed.'

He smiled sadly and nodded. 'She will not be far away, I shall bring her back; it is *she* who needs your love the most. I tried to dissuade Sir John from this course, but, as you know, he was adamant.'

It was a considerable time later that he returned. He did not have Isobel with him. 'I cannot find her; I have my staff looking both inside and out, she can't have gone far.'

Beth was sleeping on Nancy's lap and Lorna had been put to bed; her fever had returned and she was quite unwell. 'I shall get my bonnet and boots on and join in the search. Why did Sir John not offer his daughters comfort? I had not thought him a hard man, but his behaviour today was unhelpful, to say the least.'

'Lady Fenwick will be inconsolable;

Isobel is her favourite child. Today she has lost not one, but two of her daughters. As soon as we have found Isobel I shall ride over to speak to her parents again.'

Sarah snatched up her second-best bonnet, a plain chip straw with narrow brim and pale blue ribbon, and jammed it on her head. Not bothering to collect her reticule nor her gloves she dashed from her chamber to check on Lorna. Jo was sitting by the bed her eyes red and puffy.

'I'm going out with Dr Moorcroft to look for Isobel,' she whispered.

The child stirred and opened her eyes. On seeing Sarah she reached out a hand. 'Miss Shaw, please don't leave me. You're going out, I don't want you to.'

Sarah dropped to her knees beside the bed and gently smoothed the child's wrinkled forehead. 'My love, I shall not be long. Isobel is still hiding in the garden and I'm going to find her.'

'Promise me you will never leave

Beth or me. I could not bear it if you did.' Lorna's grip tightened and her eyes were huge.

Without hesitation Sarah gathered the little girl into her embrace and stroked her back lovingly. 'Of course I shall not leave you, I give you my word of honour that I will remain at Bentley Manor to take care of you as long as you have need of me.'

The fingers slackened and the little girl flopped back on the pillows with her eyes closed. Scrambling to her feet Sarah turned to the nursemaid. 'I don't know how long I shall be, hopefully Lorna will sleep until I return. Please reassure her that I am coming back just as soon as we have found her sister.'

With brimming eyes she hurried from the chamber to come face-to-face with the wonderful gentleman she'd earlier promised to marry. Taking his hand she led him to the window seat at the far end of the corridor before speaking. 'I'm so sorry, my dear, but I must ask you to release me from our engagement. I cannot marry you, I have given Lorna my word that I will stay with her indefinitely.' She couldn't look at him, hated to hurt him in this way. 'It breaks my heart to say this, but you would be better off looking for another bride. I cannot expect you to wait for me to be free to come to you, it could be many years.'

His answer was to raise her hands to his mouth and gently kiss her knuckles. 'I love you, Sarah, I will wait until you feel you are to come here as my bride, however long it takes.'

She tumbled into his arms and remained there for several minutes drawing comfort from his strength. It was he who pushed her away. 'We must not tarry, sweetheart, we must find Isobel.'

* * *

Adam somehow kept his voice even, managed not to show how hurt he was by her rejection. The children must come first in the short term, but to promise to remain with them for a decade was taking her duty too seriously. It must mean that her feelings for him were not as strong as those she had for the children, he did not want to marry a woman whose love was luke-warm. When life returned to normal Isobel found and Charlotte's funeral over, he would release her from her promise.

Thank God she had said nothing to Sir John, that only his mother knew of the arrangement. The only person to be hurt by this would be himself. He would never marry again, when he fell in love it was irrevocable. He *wished* that Sarah's feelings matched his, that he had something good to look forward to at this bleak time.

Now was not the time to dwell on this, they must find the lost girl. She had barely recovered from her illness, being outside and in such distress would do her no good at all.

* * *

It was past noon when one of the outside men discovered the missing child asleep in the hayloft. Although her face was tears streaked, her dress sadly mired, she was otherwise unharmed by her experience.

'I shall carry her back, Miss Shaw, and examine her when she's safely in her bed chamber. Don't look so concerned, she's not unconscious, just deeply asleep.'

'She looks so vulnerable, nothing like the fierce little girl I met a few weeks ago. I shall do what I can to make her last weeks with her family as happy as I can in the circumstances.'

He nodded and set off at a brisk march towards the house so that she was obliged to almost run in order to keep up with him. Something was not right between them, it was as if he had withdrawn from her. He *had* said that he was prepared to wait for her. Was he having second thoughts? She didn't blame him one jot; how could she expect such a personable gentleman to kick his heels for years waiting for his bride?

Catching up she touched his arm. 'Please, can you slow down a little. There's something I wish to ask you.' Immediately his pace slackened but he didn't glance her way. 'Isobel is not to be allowed back to Bentley Manor, but Sir John did not say she had to leave here on any particular date. Would it be possible for you to insist that the girls stay for several weeks?'

'I can do that, neither Beth nor Lorna are anything like fit enough to return. I can say that there is a risk of secondary infection, congestion of the lungs or some such nonsense.' His head turned in her direction and his lips curved slightly. 'Isobel needs time to recover her equilibrium, if she's sent away too soon it could destroy her.'

'Thank you. I'm hoping that Sir John will reconsider as his grief lessens. Lady Fenwick must want to come and visit, from what I've heard she's the most devoted mother.'

He paused, swung round to face her, Isobel held close to his heart. 'She is indeed, but like any wife she's obliged to do as her husband demands. Unless Sir John gives her permission, which I doubt that he will do, she will be forced to remain in anguish in her empty home.' His face was bleak, unshed tears glittered, he was finding this situation as difficult as she.

'We must make this a happy home for them. Together we can build up the girls spirits, persuade them all that Isobel going to school is not as bad as it seems . . .'

'You're talking fustian, Miss Shaw, and well you know it. Even little Beth understands this is the worst possible situation. For Isobel to be sent away, to be banished from her home, to not be able to see her siblings or parents for the foreseeable future . . . how can we tell them this is *not so bad?*'

His raised voice woke the sleeping child. She turned her head and seeing Sarah standing beside her reached out and clasped her hand, her voice little more than a thread. 'Miss Shaw, I should not have run away like that. I have been wicked, I killed my sister, I wish it had been I that died and not dearest Lottie.'

Sarah stepped closer and took the girl from Adam's arms. 'Sweetheart, you must not blame yourself. When you ran off it was mischievous, no more. Good heavens, a dozen or more children from the village caught measles, do you think they are blaming themselves for doing so?'

Isobel clung to her, her body convulsed with tears. 'Papa blames me, he hates me now, I can never go back.'

'Never is a long time, my love. All of you are hurting, in a few weeks things might well be different. You must be a brave girl, accept that you are going to school, but believe it will not be for ever. You must prove to your parents that you can be well-behaved, get an exemplary report, and then who knows?'

'Do you really think so, Miss Shaw? I

can be good, be kind and helpful. I will change, show everyone I am a good girl now.' She sighed and relaxed into Sarah's arms resting a wet cheek against her shoulder.

'Give her to me, it's too far for you to carry her.' Tenderly her companion reclaimed his burden and, murmuring softly, strode off leaving Sarah to follow as best she could. He said nothing further to her.

When Isobel was safely restored to her sisters Sarah waited for him to say something that would bridge the gulf between them. Instead he nodded coldly and marched out. He had made his feelings clear; his love had been a transient thing. This would make it easier to break the betrothal, she would never let him know how much she was sacrificing for the children.

8

Sarah did not have a moment to herself in the rest of the day. Eventually the three girls fell asleep, Isobel on one side of the large bed, Beth between her and Lorna. Leaving their bedroom door ajar, she retreated to her parlour where her supper tray had been waiting for an hour or more. She was shocked to discover this was not the only thing waiting for her.

'Dr Moorcroft, you startled me, I did not expect to find my *private* quarters occupied.'

He didn't beg her pardon for intruding. 'Are the children asleep?' She nodded. He stepped round her and pushed the door shut. 'What I have to say to you, Miss Shaw, would be better said in private.'

'Please, I know what it is you're going to say. There's no need for you to feel embarrassed, I release you from your obligation.'

His eyebrows crawled into his hairline and something that could have been regret flashed across his eyes. 'That is not what I wished to speak to you about. However, in the circumstances I believe that you have made the correct decision for both of us.' He turned away giving her a few moments to recover her composure.

'In which case, sir, what is it that has brought you here looking so sombre?'

He pivoted and his mouth narrowed. 'I wish to take you to task about your foolhardy promise to Isobel. How could you tell her that if she behaved herself her father would change his mind? How do you think she will feel when the other children return home for the Christmas holidays and she is obliged to remain where she is?'

Her eyes flashed. 'She must have something to hope for if she is to get through these next few weeks. It would be cruel in the extreme to let her go

143

away believing she will never return, never see her sisters or her mama again.' He might be a man of medicine, but he knew nothing about children if he believed that honesty, however brutal, was always the correct way forward.

'So, Miss Shaw, lying to children is part of your curriculum? I had thought better of you.' He rubbed his eyes as if he was in need of sleep. 'I believe it is my duty to inform the child of the truth . . . '

'You shall do no such thing, Dr Moorcroft. It's none of your concern, the children are my business and I will brook no interference.' She glared at him, daring him to contradict.

He shrugged as if the matter was of no account to him either way. 'As you wish, Miss Shaw. Pray excuse me, I have better things to do than bandy words with you.'

She watched him walk away taking all possibility of reconciliation with him. 'Stop, have you told your mother we have changed our minds, that our betrothal is at an end?'

Only then did she see the devastation in his eyes, she had mistaken the darkness for anger at her temerity in disagreeing with him. 'I was unaware until five minutes ago that you *had* changed your mind. I shall, of course, break the news.'

The door closed softly behind him, she wanted to run after him, to call him back and tell him that she loved him, that she had only broken the engagement because she thought that was why he had come to see her.

Ignoring the supper tray, she retired to bed. Her pillow was sodden before she eventually fell asleep.

★ ★ ★

Adam leant against the balustrade, he scarcely knew how he'd managed to hold back his misery. Sarah had been right, this afternoon he had all but decided to suggest they ended the arrangement. It was only when she asked to be released that he'd realised just how much he loved her. Waiting for her would have been hard, but to be without her was going to be even more difficult.

What had possessed him to berate her when they were both still raw from grieving for the loss of the little one? Matters should have been left for a few days until they had both recovered their composure. He had made a sad mull of things, behaved like a complete nincompoop and a pompous and bad-tempered one at that. She was lost to him, he might as well get used to the idea. How could he explain what had happened to his mother?

He was sorely tempted to reverse his steps and retire to his chambers without returning to the drawing-room. Mama would give him a bear-garden jaw and he would deserve it. Better to get it over and done with than have it hanging over him all night.

His mother looked up with a smile as he entered. 'At last, would you prefer tea or coffee, my dear?'

'Coffee, please.' His abrupt answer made her purse her lips but she said nothing until he was settled with the dark bitter brew on the table in front of him.

'Well, Adam? What is it you wish to tell me? Have you upset dear Sarah already?'

'Far worse. She has broken the betrothal. I behaved like a buffoon. I cannot believe I have let her slip through my fingers.' He dropped his head into his hands and could not hold back the groan of despair. To his astonishment instead of offering sympathy she laughed.

'My dear boy, of course she did. She will believe it wrong to hold you to your promise when she is not able to honour her side of the bargain, possibly for several years.'

'Are you telling me that she did this for me? That it doesn't mean she realised she did not love me enough to marry me?'

'Silly boy, you know nothing about women. You're a doctor, I am surprised you did not work this out for yourself.'

His mouth quirked. 'That's the second time tonight I've been told that. I had not thought myself an insensitive man, but if the two women in my life believe that it's so, then I suppose I must reconsider.'

'Adam, there's no such thing as a sensitive man; we womenfolk do not expect it of you. Now, drink your coffee and let's talk about how you are going to mend the fences you have broken down tonight.'

⋆ ⋆ ⋆

Sarah gathered the girls around her in what had become her refuge. A selection of old toys had been fetched from the nursery floor and three boxes of books brought up from the library. The chamber had once been used as a private parlour attached to the guest bedrooms the girls were occupying.

'Girls, it would not be appropriate to be running around in the garden today. So I propose that together we make a suitable tribute to Lottie that can be sent to your parents. Do you have any idea what she would like us to do, Isobel?'

'A picture, something like the ones you did for us when you came.' The child was sitting with one arm around Beth, the other around Lorna. 'Would you like to do that, Beth?'

'I would, but I can't draw or write my name properly.'

'What if we draw the flowers, you can colour them with your paints, and then all of you can cut them out. We can make a picture — I'm sure Mrs Moorcroft will have a box of odds and ends and perhaps some beads and buttons we can use as well.'

This suggestion was received with a modicum of enthusiasm. Satisfied the task would distract them for the majority of the day, Sarah left Nancy and Jo to prepare the room whilst she ran downstairs to make her request to Mrs Moorcroft. She would not have done this if she hadn't already seen Adam . . . no, she must not think of him in that way any more . . . had not seen Dr Moorcroft leave in the gig.

Some time during the previous day the undertakers had brought a coffin and Lottie's mortal remains were now resting in the Bentley chapel. The funeral was to be held tomorrow, only the gentlemen would attend, as was customary. Although it had been stipulated mourning was not to be worn by the children, she had fashioned armbands from black crepe for them all. She noticed, as she walked to the morning room where she hoped to find her hostess, that the servants she saw were also wearing black bands around their sleeves.

The house was unnaturally quiet, the death of a child was a dreadful thing even when the little one was not a member of your own family. She could hear voices coming from the open door ahead of her, she was not ready to be questioned by strangers. She would ask the housekeeper to find the materials she required.

Whilst she hovered uncertainly a few yards from the door it opened and the very person she least wished to meet stood before her. 'Dr Moorcroft . . . I didn't think you were here. I saw you leave on your round some time ago.'

His cheeks flushed and he smiled uncertainly. 'I apologise for startling you, Miss Shaw. I had forgotten something I needed and was obliged to return.' He ran his finger around his neck cloth as if it had become unaccountably tighter. 'How are the girls this morning?'

Flustered by his closeness she could only mumble a response. Then Mrs Moorcroft came to her rescue. 'My dear girl, come along in, don't let Adam keep you standing around in the corridor when you have obviously better things to do than talk to him.' She waved in his direction. 'Away with you, I wish to speak to Miss Shaw and you have patients to see.'

He half bowed and strode down the corridor. Sarah's pulse slowly returned to normal and she hurried into the room. 'I apologise for disturbing you, ma'am, but I am on an errand for the girls.'

In less than twenty minutes she was back in the makeshift school room, followed by a maid with an arm full of bits and bobs to make their tribute. She had been relieved that nothing had been mentioned during her brief visit about her relationship with her son. Indeed, Mrs Moorcroft had been most affable, as if nothing untoward had taken place at all.

'Here we are, girls. Mrs Moorcroft has kindly raided her treasure store, and we have enough lovely things to make a perfect picture.'

★ ★ ★

That night it took slightly less time to settle her charges and her supper tray was not waiting in her sitting room. She had almost expected to find *him* waiting for her once again and wasn't sure if she was disappointed or relieved that he was not. She wished with all her heart that she hadn't spoken so hastily, had waited until he had spoken first.

She smiled wryly; after he had delivered his tirade no doubt she would not have wished to continue the engagement anyway. Perhaps it was for the best, however much you loved a person it would be no pleasure for either party if they were constantly arguing.

The rattle of crockery approaching made her stomach rumble. She had barely eaten since . . . for a long time and was now quite ravenous. Betty had moved the pretty octagonal table so that it now stood by the open window giving her an uninterrupted view of the gardens. It was still an hour or so to sunset, when she had eaten she would take a stroll outside.

Not bothering to put on her bonnet and gloves, after all she was not leaving the grounds, Sarah slipped outside taking the back stairs. She had no wish to have an unexpected encounter with either Dr or Mrs Moorcroft. It was now dusk, the blackbirds singing their final song before they settled for the night and the nightingales not yet filling the air with their delightful chorus.

The air was heavy with the scent of roses, lavender and stocks. She inhaled deeply, then recalled the events of yesterday and felt ashamed that she'd forgotten, even for a second. Touching the armband sobered her, brought fresh tears. Botheration! She had not thought to bring a handkerchief, she would have to recourse to using her sleeve like an urchin instead or return prematurely to her chamber.

She sniffed and from a hidden arbour a ghostly hand appeared waving a large white square. 'Good heavens, sir, you frightened me half to death.' Crossly she plucked the handkerchief from his fingers, wiped her eyes and blew her nose loudly. She was sorely tempted to give him back the soiled item but restrained the impulse. He uncoiled from the stone bench. 'Miss Shaw, I do apologise for disturbing your solitude. I shall leave you to your contemplation . . . '

Something made her reach out and touch his arm. 'Please, do not go on my account. This is your house, your garden, I am the intruder here. I shall return to my chambers at once.'

'Could you not bring yourself to join me for a while? I wish to apologise for my churlish behaviour, I had no right to berate you in that fashion. My only excuse is that I was overwrought by what had happened earlier.'

'That's the third time you have apologised to me today; please, sir, could we not forget we are at odds and begin again?' No sooner were the words out than her hands flew to her mouth in horror. Would he think she was suggesting they renewed their betrothal? That was not what she had meant at all. 'I did not . . . I mean . . . you must not think . . . '

'Miss Shaw, I knew exactly what you meant. That we can be good friends as we were before. I give you my word as a gentleman I will not speak of the other matter again.'

Fresh tears brimmed, until he spoke she had not fully understood how much she wished him to ask her a second time to become his wife. He could not have made it plainer, he no longer had any wish to marry her. Regarded her as a companion with whom he could spend time; she wasn't sure she could do this without revealing her feelings. She would not become a watering pot, she was made of sterner stuff and could hide her broken heart if she had to.

'Thank you, Dr Moorcroft. If that is the case then I should be delighted to sit with you and chat for a while before I retire. Tell me, do you know how the girls' tribute was received at Bentley Manor?'

Once she was comfortably settled he replied. 'I'm afraid I have no idea, but I can tell you that my mother and I were deeply moved by the lovely item. I handed it in myself, but for some unaccountable reason I was not admitted. I should like to have checked that Lady Bentley was not suffering undue strain from the tragedy. I left my card and told the butler I intend to return tomorrow morning.'

The heady perfume of the roses that scrambled over the arbour made it difficult to think of sad things. She sighed and leant back, grateful that he had left a suitable distance between them.

'Sitting here listening to the birds and breathing in this wonderful aroma makes me think that little Charlotte has indeed gone to a better place. It's as if the Almighty is reminding us that life does not end when the spirit leaves the body, but begins a new and wonderful existence elsewhere.'

He didn't answer immediately; she could hear his rhythmic breathing, wanted to stretch out her hand and seek the comfort of his strength, but this was no longer her prerogative. She must snatch what pleasure she could from these brief interludes, enjoying his friendship and count herself blessed to be able to spend any time with the man she loved.

★ ★ ★

Adam couldn't speak, his throat was clogged with tears, he couldn't remember when he had been so moved by the loss of a patient. Sarah's words struck a chord deep in his soul, sometimes he found it hard to believe there *was* a benevolent god taking care of humankind. He saw too much suffering, too much death, in his profession to hold to his faith with any certainty.

He had so much love to give her, she was only a few feet from him, it would be so easy to reach out and draw her closer. But he would listen to his mother's advice, keep his feelings to himself until the loss of little Charlotte was less painful.

He cleared the obstruction in his throat. 'That was a wonderful thing to say, most uplifting, exactly what we both needed to hear.' He swivelled so that he was half facing her in the almost darkness. 'You must remember, however difficult things are in the next few weeks, that there's always hope. You will be happy again, I give you my word.'

He could not remain sitting so close without offering her the comfort she so obviously needed. Abruptly he stood up scattering petals over both of them as if they were emerging from the lych-gate at the village church as man and wife. He raised his head and sent up a heartfelt prayer, this was surely a sign from God that one day he would have his heart's desire.

'Shall we stroll around the garden, or do you wish to return to the house?'

'I must get back, I have been gone quite long enough. The nightingales are singing. It is hard to be downhearted when listening to them.' She shook out her skirts sending a further flurry of rose petals into the still night air. Had they reminded her also of a wedding?

9

Sarah had enjoyed her brief exchange with the doctor, she would treasure these meetings and hold them to her heart when she was obliged to leave The Rookery in a week or two. It was unlikely that she would have much contact with him when she was re-established at the children's domicile. Although there would only be two girls to teach, she would have to use all her tact and expertise to keep them focused and prevent them from dwelling on their missing sisters.

She bid her companion goodnight and hurried upstairs before he could suggest she join him for tea in the drawing room. Mrs Moorcroft had been particularly kind to her this afternoon, had donated expensive beads and scraps of lace with which the girls were able to complete their picture. She must be aware of the situation between herself and the doctor; it was strange that she had not mentioned it.

The three girls were sleeping peacefully, Nancy and Jo were talking quietly in the schoolroom. Sarah went to join them there. 'I am back now, I do not wish you to remain on duty any longer.'

Jo carefully folded the petticoat she was stitching and placed it in the mending bag. 'If you have no objection, Miss Shaw, we should like to go downstairs to the Servants' Hall. We could both do with a bit of banter, if you know what I mean.'

'It's exactly what you need. I have just spent a pleasant while in the garden talking to Dr Moorcroft.'

She regretted her comment when she saw the girls exchange glances. She must stifle these rumours before they took hold below stairs, but to make mention of the matter might just add fuel to the flames. Better to ignore the significant looks, remain aloof from personal chitchat with the staff. Being a governess was an invidious position, neither servant nor a member of the family, but somewhere suspended between the two.

The girls curtsied politely and vanished through the door that led to the back stairs. Sarah checked the room was ready for the morning, it was imperative that she kept the girls busy and turned their minds away from what would be taking place in the church just down the lane. Hopefully they would feel less distressed after the funeral. She was surprised that Lady Fenwick had not called, the children needed their mother at a time like this. A governess, especially one they had only known for such a short time, was no substitute for a loving parent.

* * *

The days passed and no word came from Bentley Manor. Both Beth and Lorna were fully recovered from their illness; it was only a matter of time before they would all have to return which would mean that Isobel must depart for boarding school.

Sarah had taken to joining Mrs Moorcroft in the drawing-room after supper leaving the two nursery maids in charge upstairs.

'My dear, I don't suppose that you've heard the latest *on dit?* Come and sit down, you look exhausted.'

'I'm not sleeping too well, ma'am, I'm dreading the summons from the Manor. Whatever I do Isobel is becoming more and more withdrawn, she spends every moment clinging to me or her sisters. She seems incapable of functioning alone.'

Mrs Moorcroft nodded sympathetically. 'Poor little thing, but what I have to tell you might well make things a little better for all of you.'

'News from Lady Fenwick?' Sarah could think of nothing else that would be of interest to her and the girls. The expected visit had not materialised, and neither had there been any written communication from either parent. This was decidedly strange.

'Yes, Adam has finally been allowed to visit her ladyship and the baby. It appears that she and Sir John are at loggerheads over his decision. I never imagined that Celia had the backbone to stand up to him. However, she has packed her bags and gone with her son to stay indefinitely with her sister in Kent.'

'Good heavens! How did she manage that? Didn't Sir John try and prevent it?'

'Celia left when he was in town on business.'

'How extraordinary, but I don't see how this removal is going to affect us.'

Mrs Moorcroft beamed. 'You are to stay here until she returns, she was most insistent on it, this means that Isobel shall not be sent away to school.'

The communicating door to the dining room was pushed open and the doctor strolled in. Although they were no longer close, spent no time alone together, at least they were good friends. She felt the colour coming to her cheeks; it was always that way when he appeared.

Adam bent down and kissed his mother's cheek and nodded to Sarah before folding himself on to a chair adjacent to hers. 'I expect that my mother has told you the good news. From what I gather Lady Fenwick is going to be away for the rest of the summer which means Isobel is safe until the autumn at least.' His expression was earnest as he continued 'I can't tell you how delighted we are that you and the girls can remain here for the next few weeks. Already this house is becoming like a happy home, I love to hear the sound of children laughing about the place.'

She smiled wryly. 'There's been little laughter lately, but we have all decided to leave off our black armbands tomorrow. It will be over a week since Charlotte died, I want the children to start enjoying themselves again. Dr

Moorcroft, would you have any objection to them making a memorial garden somewhere in your acreage? Having something to occupy them will be beneficial to their recovery.'

'Of course not, I think it an excellent idea. Mama, will you assist them in finding the ideal spot?'

'It will be my pleasure. Now, Adam, tell me what's been going on in the village today.'

'The gypsy children are now fully recovered from the disease as well, I was speaking to their leader, Jethro, he has asked me if we have any objection to them camping in our woods. The horse fair is next week and they wish to remain in the vicinity for that.'

Sarah wasn't sure she would be entirely comfortable having these exotic travellers living so close. He saw her expression and frowned. 'I thought better of you, Miss Shaw. Surely you are not prejudiced as many of the villagers? It's not the gypsies who pilfer and poach, it's the disaffected labourers and vagrants who do most of the damage.'

'Please don't worry about the gypsies, Sarah, my dear, they have stayed with us several times and I have found them no trouble at all. You would not believe how clean they keep their caravans, they would put several of the villagers to shame.'

'Will they be visible from the lawn? I don't want the girls wandering off, I'm certain that Lady Fenwick would not wish them to mingle, however, delightful they might be.'

'Mingle? I should think not, most unsuitable. I'm sure that Adam wasn't suggesting they should play with the girls, were you, dear?'

He pulled a face and laughed. 'I give in, Mama, Miss Shaw. Personally I would not think it mattered if the girls were to talk to the gypsy children sometimes, they can have no idea how privileged they are unless they see how lesser folk live.'

Sarah told Betty that Lady Fenwick had deserted her husband and children and her abigail was as shocked as she was. 'My, I can't see that it's helping Miss Isobel to run away like that, Miss Shaw.'

'Neither can I, they need to see their mother at this sad time. It might well appear to them that they have not only lost a sister, but a parent and a brother as well, if only temporarily for the latter.'

★ ★ ★

She found it difficult to sleep that night, wasn't sure whether she should tell the girls what had taken place at Bentley Manor or leave it for another week or two until they were no longer grieving for Lottie.

The matter was decided for her the next morning when the housekeeper bustled in with a thick letter. 'Miss Shaw, this has just arrived by express.

He has not waited for your reply.'

Sarah took the item with some misgivings, the only person who wrote to her was her mother and never on such fine paper or as substantial a missive as this one. The handwriting was unknown to her, with trembling fingers she snapped open the blob of red sealing wax. A thick wad of banknotes tumbled out; she stared at them in disbelief.

My dear Miss Shaw,
I am writing this in some disarray, no doubt you have heard that I left Bentley Manor in somewhat of a hurry. I wish to explain the whole to you, you must think me a poor mama to not call in to see my dear girls before I left. You will see that I have included a note for each of them which I trust you will hand over when you have read my letter.
Lord Bentley is adamant that Isobel is to blame for Lottie's death, nothing I could say would dissuade

him from that view. My eldest daughter is to be cut off from the bosom of her family, never allowed to come back, not even in the vacations.

When it became obvious my pleas and arguments were to no avail I was obliged to take matters into my own hands. Whilst he was on business elsewhere I fled Bentley Manor taking our new baby with us. I have vowed not to return until he changes his mind. I have let it be known that I am staying with my sister in Kent, but in fact I am elsewhere entirely, somewhere he will never think to look. I shall not be able to communicate again with you as he might be able to trace my letters back to me.

I have told him to place an advertisement in The Times saying that he is looking for an Estate Manager and then I shall know that not only may I return, but also Isobel, Lorna and Beth.

I trust that you will take care of my

*darlings for me until we are reunited.
Do what ever you have to do to keep
them safe. I have enclosed sufficient
funds for you to take whatever action
you see as appropriate.*

Sarah stared at the letter in disbelief.
Even if Lord Bentley could not find his
wife he could descend on The Rookery
at any time and take Isobel away. Then
the girls would be without their mother
and split asunder. It did not bear
thinking of. There must be something
she could do to prevent this.

When they had been celebrating the
fact that the girls could remain with
them throughout the summer it was
extraordinary none of them had considered the very real possibility that Lord
Fenwick would demand she return with
the girls and that Isobel leave for
school. The fact that his wife was
missing need make no difference to this
decision.

Then it became clear to her, Lady
Fenwick had sent her the money in

order that she run away with the girls, hide until the family could be reunited at some later date. Good grief! If she took the girls away without Lord Bentley's permission she could be arraigned for abduction, the penalty for that would be hanging, or transportation at the very least.

This was not a decision she could make without advice. There was only one person she would trust with the secret, and that was her erstwhile betrothed. Quickly re-folding the paper, and pushing the money into the pocket of her gown, she turned to Betty who was watching curiously.

'I must go and speak to Dr Moorcroft urgently. Betty, please tell Nancy not to take the girls out for their morning constitutional until I have spoken with them. I shall not be long.'

Her instinct was to run through the house, but commonsense prevented her. It would not do to alert the staff that there was something amiss. What she had in mind would require dissembling, and she must start that now if she was to be successful.

★ ★ ★

Adam waylaid the housekeeper as she descended the stairs. 'Mrs Taylor, I gather an express has arrived. I'm still waiting to have it given to me.'

'I beg your pardon, sir, the letter was not for you, but for Miss Shaw.'

How curious — who, that Sarah knew, could be in the position to pay the added expense of sending a letter by express delivery? He could think of only one person and his heart sank at the implication. If Lady Fenwick was in communication with Sarah in this clandestine way then it could only be because she was intending to embroil the girl in her machinations. Sir John was in no mood to brook interference from anyone in this matter. Sarah's involvement could easily end in an unmitigated disaster.

The sound of light footsteps approaching made him look up. His lips curved, he was glad she had come to him, it showed that the closeness between them was not entirely in his own imagination. He had not entirely given up hope that matters would be mended between them and eventually they could become man and wife. It would not be for want of trying on his behalf.

He moved into the shadows in order to watch her descend the staircase. The early morning sun enveloped her. A jolt of awareness almost made him stumble. How could he ever have thought her plain? Her hair, which was escaping endearingly from its severe style, had golden streaks; her beautiful eyes shone like gemstones. Even under her unflattering ensemble he could see that her figure was trim and her ankles neatly turned. She was everything he wanted in a wife.

It would not do to lurk in this unseemly manner he must step forward and speak to her. 'Miss Shaw, I have just heard you received an express delivery. I pray that it was not bad news that brings you hurrying here?'

Instead of frowning at his sudden appearance her face was illuminated by such pleasure he was almost over-whelmed. 'Adam, I must speak to you in private. I am at my wits end and have no idea how to proceed. I'm trusting that you can give me the advice I so desperately need.'

* * *

Sarah wished her intemperate words back inside her head. What would he think of her? To arrive in such disarray, her hair not properly arranged and then to use his given name? She felt unwanted heat travel from her toes to the tip of her ears. Skidding to a halt in front of him she dropped her eyes and waited for his reprimand.

'Sweetheart, I cannot tell you how glad I am that you have come to me. Come, we shall retire to my study. Not even my mother would dare disturb us there.'

A gentle finger touched her chin and raised her face so that she could see him. Her anxiety trickled away beneath the tenderness in his face. 'I beg your pardon for speaking so . . .'

'Never apologise for using my given name, my dear. We are the best of friends are we not? I intend to call you Sarah from now on, whether you give me leave or not.' He took her hand and led her down an unknown passageway and into the seclusion of his book lined study.

There was barely time to take in her surroundings; it was a substantial chamber, dominated by a massive leather topped desk. However, at the far end of the room was a small group of furniture and it was there that he guided her. 'Settle yourself, I shall have refreshments brought. You are too pale and have lost weight since you've been under my roof. As your physician I have been derelict in my duty, I intend to take better care of you from now on.'

She was grateful for the few moments his departure gave her in order to compose herself. Her heart was hammering beneath her bodice, her hands were clammy. She had not been mistaken, she was sure he returned her feelings. He loved her as much as she loved him. But would he still feel the same when she made her request? It was possible that her intentions would stretch his love to the very limits — maybe ruin her chance of happiness for ever.

He was gone for several minutes but returned carrying a laden tray. 'Here, I have hot chocolate, and coffee — I wasn't sure which you would prefer. I also have morning rolls, conserve and butter plus some ripe strawberries freshly picked from the kitchen garden. No, my dear girl, do not poker up, I shall not discuss anything with you until you have eaten.'

'Then, sir, I might as well leave now. My stomach is in turmoil, if I ate anything I would cast up my accounts on your books and I'm sure that would not be your wish.'

His chuckle warmed her. 'In which case I shall put the tray to one side and you must tell me why you are so agitated. The express was from Lady Fenwick wasn't it?' He spoke as he was selecting somewhere suitable to place the breakfast tray.

She nodded and removed the roll of bank notes from her pocket, holding them up. 'Her ladyship has asked me to take the girls away from here and keep them safe from her husband until he gives in to her demands. I fear if I don't do as she asks, Sir John might arrive and remove Isobel from my charge regardless of her mother's wishes.' She waved the money under his nose. 'I believe that I must put myself outside the law and run away with the girls using this to sustain us.'

He stared at her as if she were an escapee from Bedlam. Then the tray slipped from his hands, crashing to the floor. His expletive, as scalding coffee saturated his britches, brought colour to her cheeks.

10

'Good heavens, Dr Moorcroft, you have dropped your breakfast.'

He ground his teeth. 'Did you think I had not noticed, madam? Do not stand there like a pea goose, call for assistance.' He was ineffectually mopping at his person with his handkerchief.

Sarah looked in vain for a bell to ring. With an exclamation of disgust he stepped away from the mess and strode to the door. Flinging it open he roared down the passageway for someone to come.

An inexplicable desire to giggle bubbled up inside her. She turned her back and dropped to her knees in order to give herself something to do whilst she regained her composure. Suddenly she was back on her feet, lifted bodily from the carpet.

'Leave it, you might cut yourself on

the shards of crockery. Remain here, I shall be back within ten minutes. Order a fresh tray.'

She was impressed by his command of the situation. He was certainly adept at giving orders, but she was sure she enjoyed being on the receiving end of his dictums. She had better do as he said, she needed his advice and could not return to her chambers until she had it. The sound of servants hurrying in the direction of the study made her desirous of being seated. Fortunately she spotted the dropped money and was able to reclaim it before Mrs Taylor, followed by a bevy of female staff, arrived in the room.

With calm efficiency the housekeeper directed her girls and within minutes it was as if there had been no accident at all. It was only then that Sarah saw the hem of her gown was covered with strawberry conserve. Should she go and change it, or remain where she was until he returned? No, he might be the master of this establishment, but he was not hers. She would not sit in a soiled gown.

Betty clucked and fussed but nonetheless had Sarah's appearance fully restored within five minutes. It had even been possible to secrete the money in her reticule; but her abigail must be wondering why it was necessary to take a bag to the study. This was one piece of information she would not share with Betty, at least not until she had decided on what course of action to pursue.

As she reached the head of the staircase she saw the broad shoulders and dark hair of the doctor turning into the corridor that led to his study. Botheration! She had hoped he would take longer, now she was tardy and he would be even more cross than he had been before.

Skidding to a halt at the door she almost cannoned into him as he stepped out to look for her. 'Miss Shaw, why is it that every time I am in your vicinity some sort of calamity occurs?' His tone was playful, his eyes twinkling, he had obviously recovered from his irritation.

'I don't believe you can blame me for dropping the tray, sir, I seem to remember you were holding it at the time.' She skipped nimbly past him delighted to see that a second tray was awaiting their attention.

'Please, my dear, be seated. I am sharp set, I must break my fast before we talk. Do you think you feel well enough to join me?'

Surprisingly after all the excitement she was feeling more the thing and quite ready to eat. 'Thank you, I find that I *am* hungry now. I'm sorry I was absent when you returned, I was forced to return to my chamber to repair my appearance.'

He grinned sheepishly as he arranged freshly baked scones, butter and conserve on a plate for her. 'I apologise most humbly for barking at you. My only excuse is that my leg was smarting, I fear I did not notice you had as much need as I to change your raiment.'

Somehow her hand had reached over the table and was resting on his. 'I do hope you were not seriously scalded? If I had thought, I would have thrown that vase of flowers on your leg. I'm surprised, as a medical man, that you did not suggest it yourself.'

His unexpected shout of laughter startled her. 'Good heavens, I'm fortunate that you did not. But, you are quite right, cold water is exactly the right thing for a burn of any sort. I'm surprised that you know such a thing.'

'Before my papa passed away, he was a pastor, you know, I was encouraged to accompany the local physician on his rounds. He was a good doctor, open-minded when it came to new practices; if I had been born a gentleman I'm certain I would have become a doctor myself.' Quickly removing her hand, she busied herself spreading butter on the still warm scone.

'And an excellent one you would have made; perhaps one day in the future it will be possible for women to join our ranks. I, for one, do not hold with the view that females are an inferior species and lack the intelligence to do the same work as a man.'

What an extraordinary conversation to be having at such a time as this? Did he think she was a radical, like Mrs Wollstonecraft, that she supported Lady Fenwick's desertion? She paused as she raised her food to her mouth. 'I don't wish you to think that I am in favour of a wife deserting her husband as a matter of course when things become difficult. Both parties make a solemn promise in the sight of God when they are married. The wife promises to honour and obey, so I believe that she ought to do so if she can.'

He nodded as if in agreement. 'From your words, my dear, I take it you think there are exceptions to this rule?'

Her mouth was full, she could not answer until she had swallowed. Smiling in her direction he poured her a large bowl of hot chocolate. She wished she'd asked for coffee now, slurping was not something she wished to do in front of him.

'Lady Fenwick would not have abandoned Sir John if she had not been driven to it by his intransigence. We both know it wasn't Isobel's fault that Lottie died, she does not deserve to be punished at all, let alone be sent away for ever. I'm sure when his grief is less he will reconsider.'

'I beg to disagree. I have known Sir John for three years now, he's not a clever man, but is certainly one to bear grudges. It would take nothing short of a miracle to make him change his mind. All Lady Fenwick is doing by her absence is hardening his resolve. However he won't be arriving to take Isobel from us. At this moment he is gallivanting across the countryside in his search for his errant wife.'

Her appetite suddenly vanished. Even the hot chocolate no longer seemed appetising. In fact the further she was from the tray the more comfortable she'd feel. 'I shall leave you to finish your breakfast, I'm no longer hungry. However, if you'd be so kind as to bring me a cup of coffee when you're done, I should be most grateful.'

The knife he was holding clattered on to the plate. 'Go and sit by the window, I'll bring your drink immediately.'

Sarah selected an upright bentwood chair which was light enough for her to carry to the open window. This was already pushed up to its fullest extent, and there was an ample sill upon which to place the coffee when it came. The fresh air soon revived her, settled her normally docile digestion.

'Too much excitement can play havoc with one's equilibrium, Sarah. I don't like to see you so discommoded . . . ' he placed her drink within easy reach of her hand and brought up a similar chair placing it rather close to hers. 'My love, it would make things so much simpler if I did have the right to take care of you. Please, can I ask you to reconsider your decision?'

This was exactly what she'd dreamt of hearing, he wished to become affianced to her once more. She was about to tell him there was nothing she would like better when doubts assailed her. He had not said what it was he wished her to reconsider — she had no wish to embarrass herself, or him by then answering in the affirmative a question he had not actually asked.

'Sarah, sweetheart, am I mistaken? Is your hesitation a sign that you no longer have feelings for me? No longer wish to become my wife at some time in the future?'

Joy flooded through her. She raised her face, unable for a moment to reply. 'Dr . . . Adam, my feelings have not changed one iota. I love you with all my heart, and if you are still prepared to take me as your betrothed knowing it could be a considerable time before we can be together, then I am happy to become your responsibility.'

His fingers closed over hers and gently drew her to her feet. His arms encircled her, she leant her face against his chest and could hear his heart thumping beneath his snow white shirt front. He was as moved as she by the moment. Shyly she looked up and he responded by placing his lips on hers. This sweet gesture sealed the bond between them.

Then he briskly moved his chair to the far side of the window, swinging it round he straddled it and folded his arms across the chair back. She returned to her seat, everything was changed. Whatever happened she believed one day she would be his wife, that was all that mattered.

The cup rattled in the saucer and she took a few sips of the dark aromatic brew. The bitterness cleared her head as nothing else could. Replacing the item on the window sill she smiled across at him. 'Well, how is this matter to be resolved?'

'Firstly I shall send a letter after Sir John telling him that Isobel and Lorna have suffered a setback, that they are in no condition to return to Bentley Manor.'

She waited expectantly for him to continue, he raised an eyebrow and she giggled. 'I beg your pardon, I did not realise I was supposed to comment. Such a missive will give us valuable time, but this is not a solution. Either I break the law or disobey my employer's instructions; in either case I shall certainly lose my position.'

'I can't say that I would be sorry if that happened, it would mean we could be married immediately.' He raised a hand placatingly as she drew breath to protest. 'I know, my dear, it might be beneficial to us but disastrous to the children. We must put their needs first, for the moment at least.'

'Is that your only suggestion? It does not solve the problem of how to keep Isobel safe until matters improve between Sir John and Lady Fenwick.'

'My suggestion is that you take the girls to the seaside in order for them to convalesce. If you do it on my advice, and we let Sir John know that I am now your betrothed, he can have no objection to your going.'

'My mother is living in Poole, a small town in Dorset.'

'Excellent. You must write to her at once, tell her the situation and ask if you and the girls can stay with her for the rest of the summer.'

'I can't do that, she is the unpaid companion to an elderly relative; even if the house were large enough, I should not wish to take the girls there.'

He paced the room, she noticed he walked with his eyes shut. A dangerous habit, especially when she'd been obliged to move his furniture around. Abruptly he halted and bounded back to sit down once more. 'I have it; I shall send Fred Burton, my estate manager, to your mother's dwelling. He must collect her and together they can find a suitable house to rent for the remainder of the summer. Mrs Shaw must engage the necessary staff, and make things ready for you. My mother can accompany you and the girls on the journey.'

Her head was spinning, she could hardly take in what he said. 'We are to live in Dorset? My mother will not be able to go back . . . '

'I know that, I told you things would be simpler if I am your betrothed. What could be easier than my taking on the responsibility of your only relative? When we return here she will, of course, accompany us.'

There was one small flaw in his plan. 'But, Adam, what about yourself? Are you to remain here in this house all alone?'

'Certainly not, I have one or two business, and medical matters, to attend to before I can leave. But be assured, darling girl, I shall join you as I'm able. I have not taken a break from my work since I qualified, it will do me good to be away for a while.'

'But what of your patients? How will they go on without you?'

'There is an excellent apothecary in

the village, also two good-wives in the neighbourhood who already deliver the majority of the babies. I shall speak to Dr Jeffries, a colleague of mine in the next town, I'm sure he will take on any urgent cases in my absence.'

Sarah drained her coffee. 'In which case I shall return to my chamber to compose my letter, I . . . '

'Do it here, there's ink and paper on the desk. Burton will be in the office, I shall go and speak to him directly. Can you have your missive completed within fifteen minutes?'

'Easily, and another thing, I must give you the money Lady Fenwick sent me. I haven't dared to count it, but it seems a vast amount. I shudder to think what she was obliged to do in order to obtain so much without her husband's knowledge.'

His hand shot out to catch the roll of notes. He flicked through it. 'There must be £200 at least, I shall put it in the safe and return it when Lady Fenwick is in residence again.'

Whilst she was penning the letter she felt ashamed of the happiness that ran through her. It was wrong to feel like this so soon after the death of Charlotte. She must make sure she kept her feelings to herself, it would not do to upset the girls. She would tell them, and the staff that it was an engagement of convenience in order that Adam could legitimately take charge of her welfare.

They were both hoping society in general, and Sir John in particular, would consider it acceptable that Adam took responsibility for the girls as well as herself. The fact that Sir John was no longer in the neighbourhood, and there were no other male relatives to step into his shoes in his absence, should be enough to smooth things over.

It must be made very clear to both her mama, and his, that it was a business arrangement. Her mama would think it nonsensical to be engaged to a man with no limit to the time before the actual nuptials took place. It was another matter entirely to convince Adam this was the best way forward. *He* must desist at once in larding his conversation with endearments, *she* must attempt to remain unmoved when he was nearby.

Up to an hour ago they had behaved as friends when they were together, keeping their feelings obscured behind good manners. Hiding their love was going to be more difficult, but if they were to put the girls' welfare before their own, then it must be done.

Explaining to her mother, without revealing how she felt about Adam, was harder than she'd expected. Even writing that it was an engagement without substance, one that would be broken off when matters resolved themselves at Bentley Manor, was upsetting. It was the first time she had ever deliberately misled her parent, she prayed that when her beloved mama eventually discovered the truth she would understand.

Within the hour Mr Burton had left on the long journey to Dorset. He was to travel by post, exorbitantly expensive, but Adam had insisted it was imperative matters were arranged speedily.

'I shall send you all in my travelling carriage, it has recently been resprung and one of Burton's tasks is to arrange your overnight accommodation and to have a fresh team waiting at each post house. With luck you shall be on your way by the beginning of next week.'

Now was the moment she'd been dreading, she must persuade him to agree to her deception. 'Adam, I have told my mother we have become engaged solely to give you the right to take care of us. In other words, it's a business arrangement, one that will be dissolved when matters right themselves between Sir John and Lady Fenwick.' She braced herself for his angry denial.

Instead his mouth curved and he touched her cheek lightly with one finger. 'Exactly what I was going to suggest, sweetheart. Time enough to reveal our love when we are in a position to act upon it. We must continue as before; it's going to be the hardest part of this tangle. Every time I see you I want to hold you, I want to shout from the tallest mountain how happy I am that the most wonderful girl loves me as much as I love her.'

He opened his arms and she walked in; it was where she belonged, where she felt safe and loved. Women who were married to seafaring men or soldiers often only saw their menfolk for a month or two every other year. At least she would have the blessing of his company, be able to talk to him whenever she wished.

This time it was she who stepped away. 'All that matters, my love, is that the girls are safe and happy. We must pray that something persuades Sir John to change his mind about sending Isobel away. If that happens then it will be the first step to our being together.'

11

Within three days a note arrived by express for Dr Moorcroft, from Mr Burton, saying that a suitable house had been leased and everything would be ready for their arrival by the end of the week. He beamed at Sarah. 'My word, your mother's a marvel. How she has accomplished so much in less than a day I cannot imagine.'

'I am certain that being freed from her servitude so unexpectedly will have given her the necessary vigour to achieve the impossible. Did Mr Burton say what kind of house she has found?'

'Read it yourself, my dear. Mama says your packing is all but done, the baggage must leave this morning, you can depart the day after tomorrow. That should be ample time. I'm sure you would not wish to arrive before your belongings. Have you decided which of the girls will accompany the trunks?'

Sarah looked up from the brief letter with a smile. 'How typical of a man to write so little upon the subject that is so vital to our well-being. 'The house is substantial and no more than a stone's throw from the sea.' I am already consumed with curiosity and must now wait until I see this place for myself.'

As they were alone in his study they were able to be more relaxed than would otherwise be possible. He shook his head in mock despair. 'My love, you have not answered my question. Will you be ready to leave in two days and who is to leave today?'

'Both Nancy and Jo are going, you have more than sufficient staff to do their duties until we leave. Betty is to act as abigail to both your mother and myself, she will travel in the carriage with us.'

'It's a journey of almost one hundred and fifty miles, you do not want to be cramped. My new travelling carriage is luxurious, but three children and three adults will be a tight squeeze.' He closed his eyes and she barely resisted the urge to reach out and touch him. She loved the way his forehead creased whilst he was thinking. 'I shall hire a second carriage, then Mama may take her own dresser and Mrs Shaw can then share Betty with you.'

'Oh, the expense will be dreadful. We can manage . . . '

Her protests were silenced by a light kiss. 'I believe there's something you are not aware of, you're obviously under the misapprehension that I am living in straitened circumstances. My father made a fortune in India, and I am an extremely wealthy man.'

Her mouth opened, she felt as if the stone had lodged in her chest. This was not good news, for him to marry a governess when he was merely a village doctor was just acceptable. For a wealthy man, an extremely wealthy man, to do so would be considered a misalliance by society.

She mumbled something appropriate

and begged to be excused, she was almost at the door when he stepped in front of her blocking her passage.

'Now, my darling, you understand why I did not tell you this. I knew you would think yourself an unsuitable match and run away.'

She stared firmly at her slippers refusing to answer or look up. His hand cupped her chin and gently raised it until she was staring into his strange eyes. 'You are the daughter of a parson, well-educated and quite definitely a member of the gentility. That you are obliged to work as a governess is to your credit not your shame. I know what you're thinking, that it will somehow damage my reputation.'

'You know that's true; I should have realised by the size of your house and the fact that you have an estate manager. It did not occur to me that you're a man of substance, you dress simply and live without ostentation.'

His smile made her toes curl in their slippers. He was irresistible when he

looked at her like this. 'Exactly so, sweetheart. I am not extravagant, I only employ so many staff in order to give folk work. I bought a large estate for the same reason. I work because medicine interests me, it gives purpose to my days.' His hands transferred to her shoulders and gently squeezed. 'I love you, and don't give a fig for society. If I had fallen in love with your abigail instead of you I should not have hesitated to marry her. I am wealthy enough to please myself and disregard the opprobrium of others.'

Betty was old enough to be his mother, the thought of him offering for her made her smile. Blinking back her tears she stretched out and kissed him. His shock was laughable. 'If you would prefer to transfer your affections to Betty, then please do not mind me.' She stepped away from him and looked pointedly at the door.

'You, if you will forgive me for saying so, my darling, are an impertinent baggage. I can see that I shall have to

take you in hand once we're mar.
He scowled ferociously and opened
door. She could hear him laughing
she ran upstairs to give instructions t
the trunks to be carried down immedi
ately.

Even Isobel became more animated
when she was told they would be
departing in two days. 'How long will
the journey take, Miss Shaw? Shall we
all be travelling in the same carriage?'

'We shall be stopping overnighting
three times, Mr Burton has reserved
our accommodation. Dr Moorcroft is
sending two carriages, so we shall have
ample room.'

Lorna put her arm around her twin.
'Bella, we shall be gone before Papa
returns. You shall not be sent away to
school, you shall stay with us as Mama
wishes you to.'

It was a delight to see how Lorna had
blossomed over the past few days, *her*
confidence had grown as her more
dominant sister had retreated into her
shell. Hopefully a happy balance would

eventually be achieved where the sisters would be equal.

Later that morning when the baggage vehicle was leaving the girls asked to go downstairs in order to wave them off. 'I shall ask Cook to send us an alfresco luncheon. We should be spending as much time as possible outside whilst the weather is so good.'

Beth insisted on taking the message, Lorna accompanied her to make sure the little girl did not get lost in the rabbit warren of passages that made up the servants' quarters. Isobel gripped her hand and stared up, her thin face etched with worry.

'Miss Shaw, what is to happen to me? Whatever you say, I know that Lottie would not have caught the measles but for my disobedience. Mama would not have run away either. The family has fallen apart, and it's all my fault. I think it would be better if I went away to school, at least then Beth and Lorna and Mama and baby John could return to Bentley Manor.'

'Bella, you must not think like this. The rift between your parents, although on the face of it caused by a disagreement over whether you should be sent away to school, is more about Sir John's grief. It is this that has made him overly harsh.'

She gathered the trembling child in her arms and took her to the window seat. Isobel was really too old to sit on her lap, but today she needed the physical comfort of being held close by a loving adult. Sarah was shocked how light the girl was; how could she have lost so much weight in such a short time?

'Darling, listen to me. Whatever you might think, both your parents love you very much. They are grieving sorely the loss of your sister, as are we all. The best thing you can do is get well, so whatever happens in the autumn you will be strong enough to deal with it.'

'I don't have to go to school right now?'

Sarah hugged the child tighter. 'You

don't, you need a complete break, you're very run down after your illness. A few weeks in the sunshine at the seaside will restore you. When we come back in September, if Sir John still wishes you to go away, you will be ready to do it with good grace. School might seem like a punishment, but I thoroughly enjoyed my time there.'

'But Lorna and I have never been apart, it's not like an ordinary girl going, is it? We are twins, we share a special bond.'

'I know, it will be very difficult for both of you. But I'm sure once your papa sees that you are a changed girl, not the headstrong child you were, he will wish to have you back in the bosom of the family. I applaud your sentiments, my dear, but you must put your parents difficulties to one side. It's no concern of yours, or mine, so you must go to the seaside and concentrate on getting well. Can you do that for me, Isobel?'

'I can, Miss Shaw. You're the nicest

person I've ever met, as long as you're here to take care of me I know I shall be safe.' She wriggled from Sarah's lap and knelt on the window seat to stare earnestly into her eyes. 'Promise me, Miss Shaw, that you'll never leave me?'

Sarah had no choice. 'I give you my word, Isobel, that as long as I'm needed I shall be there.' With this second promise, she was doubly committed.

Satisfied with this answer the girl bounced down and ran after her siblings; it was as if she had discarded a heavy load, could be a normal child once more. If only life were so simple. Isobel, having been reassured that Sarah would not abandon them, was ready to face the world. What of herself? From whatever angle she viewed the situation she could see only heartbreak ahead for her and Adam. It was possible she would be held to her vow until Isobel came out; as the child was only nine years of age, this meant it could be that many years before she and Adam could finally tie the knot.

What man, however loving, would be prepared to wait so long? At some point she was going to have to break her word to either Isobel or Adam. She shuddered; her name day was next month, she would be three and twenty. Already several of her friends from the Petersham Academy for Young Ladies had children. The thought that she might have to wait until she was past her thirtieth birthday before holding a baby of her own was not a happy prospect.

Today was not the time to brood, she must put aside her sadness. Neither Adam nor the children must ever know how torn she was between duty and love. No doubt her mother would have much to say on the matter as well. Thinking about their reunion raised her spirits, it was almost two years since they had seen each other. Exchanging regular letters was no substitute for being able to hold her beloved parent in her arms.

* * *

The time for their departure eventually arrived. Tom Coachman and the head groom were on the box of the smart new travelling carriage that Sarah and the children were to use. Mrs Moorcroft and her maid were to use the second, smaller vehicle. This meant the three girls could occupy one seat and Betty and herself the other. The necessary carpetbags containing what would be needed on the journey were safely stowed with Mrs Moorcroft.

Adam was there to wish them well. 'The house is going to seem sadly empty when you're gone, sweetheart.'

'I had not realised I took up so much space, my dear. Surely it's the children and your mother you will miss the most?' Her sally had the desired effect and his expression lightened.

'My darling, you might be small in size but our love fills the house with happiness in a way that no amount of other people could. I shall be counting the hours until I can join you in Dorset.'

They were standing a discreet distance apart, she knew he wanted to embrace her as much she wished to feel his arms around her. Being obliged to pretend what was between them was merely friendship was becoming more difficult by the day. At least when he was absent she would have no need to dissemble.

'I do believe I'm as excited as the children, I have never seen the sea. One day I should like to sail across to France, or perhaps along the coast and into the Mediterranean.' She sighed and he stepped closer.

'I promise, my love, that day will come. I shall purchase a yacht and take you anywhere you wish to go for our wedding trip. Since we beat the French at Waterloo and that upstart Napoleon Bonaparte has been incarcerated on St Helena, it's possible to travel anywhere on the continent without danger.' His eyes burned into hers, she was mesmerised.

A call from the coach came just in

time to avert what would have been a disaster. For them to have embraced in full view of everyone would have revealed their secret instantly.

'Miss Shaw, are you coming? Will you please sit next to me?'

Laughing she raised her hand in farewell and ran to the waiting groom who handed her into the carriage and neatly flicked the steps into place before closing the door. The windows had been let down; it was going to be a long, hot journey and Sarah had decided it would be better to be covered in dust than without fresh air.

★   ★   ★

'Are we there yet, Miss Shaw? You said it was not much further and that was ages ago,' Lorna said plaintively. Unfortunately she had proved to be a poor traveller, whereas little Beth and Isobel had revelled in every bounce and jolt, screeching with laughter when the carriage lurched from side to side.

'Normally I do not approve of children hanging out of the carriage window, however in your case I shall make an exception, Lorna. You must come over to my side, hold on to the window frame and look forward and tell me what you see.'

Reluctantly the girl did as requested. Beth was fast asleep her head in Isobel's lap. A few weeks ago the girl would have tipped her little sister onto the floor and pushed Lorna out of the way in order to be first to look out of the window. She was a changed child, the shock of her sister dying so suddenly had brought the sweetness of her disposition to the forefront. There was not an hour had passed in which Isobel did not show her siblings kindness.

'I don't like standing up, Miss Shaw, I fear I shall be ill again.'

'Nonsense, Lorna, do as I say and you will be glad that you did.' Sarah shifted forward on the squabs and put a steadying arm around the girl.

The girl edged closer until she was leaning on the door itself. Cautiously she leant out through the open window and turned her head to stare to the front. Her body stiffened and she screamed in delight. Beth jerked sideways and fell into the well of the carriage taking Isobel with her in a flurry of arms and legs.

Lorna spun round no longer bothered by the movement of the vehicle. 'Bella, Beth, come and look. It's so big, it goes on for ever. I've never seen anything like it.'

Unbothered by their tumble the other two scrambled up and joined her in the window. Sarah lifted Beth as she was too small to lean out without assistance. The sea stretched in rippling waves as far as the eye could see, reflecting the blue sky above, making the water seem turquoise, magical. She had been watching it for several miles, had been as entranced as they were.

'Well, girls, do you think it worth it now to have come all this way?' There had been several moments over the past three days when not only the children, but herself, had wondered if such an arduous journey was really worth the effort. One glance at the water and her doubts had fled.

Lorna and Isobel were bouncing up and down with excitement, Beth was becoming agitated because she could not see it as well as her older sisters. Sarah was about to suggest that one of the girls gave way so that Beth could be held at the window when Isobel turned.

'Come along, nuisance, let me hold you in the window and then you can see properly.'

Beth flung herself into Isobel's arms and was soon crowing with delight. 'I can see the sea. See the sea. See the sea.'

Lorna rushed to the other side and looked backwards. 'And I can see the other carriage, it's a long way back, but I'm sure it's them.'

Mrs Moorcroft had also proved to be a dreadful passenger, it had taken both maids to take care of her. The girls had behaved impeccably making Sarah's task an easy one.

'Good, with luck we will arrive before them and that will give me time to warn the staff to have a bedchamber prepared for Mrs Moorcroft. I'm sure she will recover from her sickness as soon as she is out of the carriage.'

'I wasn't sick, was I, Miss Shaw?'

'No, Beth, you weren't. Poor Lorna was the only one so afflicted, and, thank God, she was not as poorly as Mrs Moorcroft.'

'I feel much better now I know we're almost there. Can we go down to the beach straightaway? Shall we be able to bathe? Beth and I cannot swim, but Isobel can.' Lorna gulped and then continued softly. 'Lottie was the best swimmer, she would have loved to come to the seaside with us.'

Sadness filled the carriage, the girls slunk back on to the seats in silence. 'Lottie has gone to heaven, but she is not lost to us. As long as we love her in our hearts she will be close by, sharing our lives. You will all be reunited one day. She would not wish you to be sad on such a happy day.'

Three blonde heads nodded but Isobel and Lorna slid in closer to Beth and they didn't answer. It was going to take the rest of the summer with them to come to terms with their loss, Sarah prayed the change of scene would be enough to begin the healing process.

The letter that had caught up with them that morning had filled her with foreboding. Adam had said that Sir John had discovered where his wife was hiding and was going to collect her at this very moment. How long this would take was unclear, but certainly it meant that their time at the seaside might be abruptly cut short. An irate Sir John could descend on them demanding they should return forthwith; or, even worse, send Isobel away to school before she had time to fully recover.

12

The carriage trundled through the small market town of Poole and on into the countryside. Eventually it turned through imposing gates and down an immaculate drive to pull up in the turning circle in front of a modern edifice. Sarah turned to her maid who had rejoined her in the carriage.

'Betty, this looks like a new building. I wonder why the owners are not living in it themselves.'

'I reckon it was built for a newly married couple; maybe the wife died or the engagement was broken. What I do know, Miss Shaw, that it must have cost a pretty penny to rent it. It's easily as large as Bentley Manor and the grounds are magnificent.'

Sarah scarcely heard this comment, her eyes were fixed on the small, plump figure waving from the top step.

It was her mama, she couldn't wait to descend from the carriage and embrace her. Beth grabbed her elbow impatiently.

'Miss Shaw, Miss Shaw, who's that waving to us?'

'That's my mother, Beth, it's she has found this wonderful house for us. She's going to be living with us whilst we're at the seaside.' They didn't need to know that her mama would be living with Adam and his mother when she and the children returned to Bentley Manor in the autumn.

'You go on ahead, miss, I'll see to the little ones.'

Sarah was out of the carriage without waiting for the steps to be lowered, gathering up her skirts in one hand, she ran to greet her mother. 'I can't tell you how pleased I am to see you, my dear girl, but you are too thin. I shall make it my business to restore the sparkle to your eyes and the roses to your cheeks whilst we're living here.'

'Mama, you look so well. The girls

are coming in with Betty; did our luggage arrive safely?'

With linked arms she stepped into the capacious entrance hall. She stared in awe at the expanse of chequered floor, at the staircase which curved around the wall on either side of the circular hall. Light flooded in through the floor-to-ceiling windows, it was a stunning space. 'I am impressed, Mama, where did you find such a place, and in so short a time as well?'

'It was built for a young couple, but the gentleman was killed in a riding accident and his widow has returned to her parents to grieve. They were only in occupation for a few months before the tragedy.'

A homely woman hurried up to greet her, her navy blue bombazine rustling as she walked. She curtsied politely. 'Stubbing, at your service, Miss Shaw. The nursery floor is ready for the young ladies, your chamber, and that of Mrs Moorcroft is also prepared.'

'Mrs Moorcroft has had a wretched

journey, she will need to retire immediately. Her carriage will be here within the next half an hour. Please ensure the shutters and drapes are drawn and the bed turned down.'

'I shall see to it at once, madam. Do you wish to go to your apartment?'

'No, thank you, I shall make sure the girls are comfortable and then Mrs Shaw must show me around. I should like tea to be served in the nursery in an hour, if you please. I shall require nothing other than fresh lemonade, if that is possible.'

The housekeeper nodded, bobbed again, and vanished with a swish of her skirts. 'Stubbing seems an efficient and pleasant woman, Mama. How did you find her so quickly?'

'The house came fully staffed, we have a superfluity of footmen, a pompous butler, who fortunately is indisposed today, and more parlour maids and chambermaids then we shall ever have need for. But Mr Burton insisted Dr Moorcroft wished to take on everyone, it would seem your young man has very deep pockets, my dear.'

Sarah flushed. 'I thought I explained to you, in my letter, that it's a business arrangement between us, not a genuine engagement. I'm committed to working with the Bentley family for the next few years, I could not possibly enter into a genuine betrothal, now could I?'

Her mother smiled knowingly but held her peace. There was no further opportunity for private conversation as the children erupted into the house exclaiming loudly at everything they saw. Nancy appeared to greet them, and they flung themselves at the girl as if they'd been parted for weeks and not days.

'Shall I take them up, Miss Shaw? It's ever so nice upstairs, I've never seen the like. I'm not sure about the indoor closet, can't fathom how it works, but the bathing room is a wonder to behold. Imagine not having to carry all that dirty water downstairs?'

Smiling, Sarah waved the girls away.

'Run along, Jo is waiting for you upstairs. Make sure they change into something clean, wash their faces and hands, Nancy. After tea please bring them downstairs and we shall go and explore the beach.'

Chattering like magpies the girls vanished with their nursery maid. Isobel as vocal as the others, it was a pleasure to see her so ebullient after the past weeks of almost silence. 'Mama, what is all this about indoor plumbing? I've never seen anything of that sort, please take me at once to view this marvel of engineering.'

It was a mystery to her where the soiled water went; a small plug was removed from the aperture in the base of the bath and it would seem that the contents vanished through it never to be seen again. The water closet was even more remarkable, but she viewed it with some suspicion, and could see why Nancy had her reservations. However, anything that made life easier for the servants was a good thing, in her opinion. Carrying buckets full of dirty water, or night soil, could not be a pleasant experience.

Her chambers were light and airy, her private parlour even had a small balcony upon which she could sit and eat her breakfast looking out to sea. These rooms were far too grand for someone as lowly as a governess, but her mother insisted she was entitled to have the best as she was engaged, however irregular the arrangement, to the master of the house.

The remainder of the day passed pleasantly enough, the children were enchanted with the beach, but by the time they all returned from their excursion Sarah had decided that sand was not something she enjoyed having stuck between her toes. In future the girls could paddle, explore the rock pools and build castles made of sand with the help of their maids, an arrangement that suited them all.

An alfresco supper was served, (high tea had been substituted for dinner), and Mrs Moorcroft felt sufficiently recovered to join her mother and herself on the terrace.

'My dear Sarah, I do believe you have freckles already. You must remember to keep on your bonnet if you venture to the beach again tomorrow.'

'I'm remaining here, the girls can play by the sea with Nancy and Jo. I cannot see the attraction, myself; the water is freezing and the sand gets everywhere. I shall admire the panorama from the safety of the terrace in future.'

Both matrons chuckled. 'I entirely agree with you, Sarah, sand and sea shells are best left to children. I cannot tell you how pleased I am to be here, it was a wretched journey, the thought of having to endure it in order to return in the autumn quite fills me with trepidation.'

Sarah's mother smiled sympathetically. 'I do so sympathise, Mrs Moorcroft. Have you tried . . . '

The two ladies chatted happily

leaving Sarah to her reverie. It was quite possible their interlude in the sunshine of Dorset might be brought rudely to a halt if Sir John discovered their whereabouts. At least they ought to have at least a week to enjoy the tranquillity before having to worry about his unwanted arrival.

'Well, Sarah, what do you think?'

'I beg your pardon, Mama, I was wool-gathering. Could I ask you to repeat your question?'

'We thought a spring wedding would be ideal; that will give you and Dr Moorcroft ample time to further your relationship. It will also allow the girls to recover from their loss and for Lady Fenwick to find a suitable replacement.'

★　★　★

Adam scanned the message that had arrived from the man he had sent to follow Sir John's progress around the countryside. Excellent, Sir John had succumbed to a severe case of gout and was unable to continue his journey to fetch Lady Fenwick.

Mrs Taylor coughed to draw his attention. Good grief, the poor woman had been waiting to speak to him for several minutes. 'How can I help you?'

'The holland covers have been put over all the furniture in both your apartment and the apartments as Miss Shaw will use when you are married. The wallpaper you selected has arrived from London, the men are waiting to start redecorating.'

'They are — that's splendid. The post chaise will arrive to collect me in the next half an hour. Arrange for my trunk to be brought down, if you please, then the men can begin the renovations.'

Smiling at the thought of Sarah's reaction when she returned to see her future chambers were freshly painted, the bed hangings and curtains replaced and a newfangled bathing room and water closet installed for her personal use.

She might not be so sanguine about

the fact he'd not followed her instructions on the matter of their future
nuptials. As far as his staff, and his
mother, were aware it was a genuine
engagement, a love match, and the
wedding would take place some time
the following year. He was rather
hoping that she would feel obliged to
marry him whatever her reservations
about leaving the children when she
saw how happy everyone was at the
prospect of her becoming the mistress
of The Rookery.

'I'm expecting Burton to arrive at
any moment, see that he joins me in my
study directly he appears.'

His housekeeper curtsied and vanished back to her duties. He had a
particular errand for Burton, one that
he hoped would delay the inevitable,
give them all a summer without upset.
His estate manager arrived and Adam
gestured that he sat in the chair on the
other side of the vast desk. 'Burton, I
have a letter here explaining to Sir John
that I have taken his daughters to

Dorset in order for them to make a complete recovery from their illness. However, I wish you to send a reliable minion to chase after him.'

'You don't want the letter to reach him for several weeks?'

'Exactly; it must arrive at each of the places he had visited and then follow him. No doubt he will have returned to Bentley Manor with Lady Fenwick long before my missive catches up with him. No one here, apart from yourself, has the location of our summer residence. All the staff know is that we have moved to the seaside.'

His man nodded. 'By the time he fathoms out where you are you'll be on your way back. I'll make myself scarce if he comes calling, make sure I don't have to lie.'

'Good man, I knew I could rely on your discretion. I wish you to oversee the renewals and renovations that are being done in my absence. Mrs Taylor is to spring clean the entire house, that will occupy the staff for the remainder of the summer.'

'I understand that everyone is to have time off to visit relatives, I doubt that any other master in the county would treat his people so well.'

The crunch of carriage wheels on the gravel outside the window reminded Adam that he was about to leave for Dorset himself. 'You know where you can contact me if necessary, I am relying on you, Burton, to ensure the changes are done without mishap.'

Twenty minutes later he was comfortably ensconced in the chaise that would convey him to the next Post house. There would be a fresh team waiting on his arrival; his intention was to complete the journey in half the time it had taken the ladies. It had been a long week without sight of the woman he loved. He would have his own horses available to him when he arrived and Burton had rented a gig for his use.

★ ★ ★

Sarah's jaw dropped, surely Adam should have explained to both of them that this was a fabricated arrangement? That no wedding would take place in the future, or maybe at all. 'There's been some mistake, we cannot be married next year. I gave my word to the girls that I would stay with the family as long as I was needed. I have no intention of going back on this promise.'

Instead of this news been greeted with consternation the women exchanged glances. It was her mother who spoke first. 'By next spring the girls will no longer require you to be constantly at their side, children are resilient creatures they will have moved on.'

Shocked that they didn't understand how difficult it was for her to have chosen the girls over her own happiness, Sarah jumped to her feet. 'Knowing that I am with her sisters, taking care of them in her absence, will be essential for Isobel's peace of mind. Adam is well aware that I'm not free to marry him, we have agreed it will be an engagement of indefinite length.'

'Fustian, my dear girl, if ever I heard it,' Mrs Moorcroft exclaimed. 'Whatever my son might have said to you, he's already having the house redecorated, your personal apartment refurbished, in the full expectation that you will be man and wife next year.'

Sarah's concern turned to anger. He had no right to ride roughshod over her wishes in this way, to discuss their plans with anyone but herself, and certainly not with his mother first. Stiffly she nodded to both women. 'If you will excuse me, ma'am, Mama, I no longer have an appetite. I have a deal of hard thinking to do, it will be best if I do it in the solitude of my own chamber.' Not waiting for either of them to remonstrate, she marched off towards the house her back rigid, bristling with indignation.

* * *

The next few days she spent all her time with the children; braving the nasty sand and cold seawater was preferable to being taken to task by her mother and Mrs Moorcroft. Her meals were eaten in the nursery, she remained upstairs until after they went inside. Only then could she be certain she would not be accosted when venturing into the gardens. Anyway, it was far better to walk in the dusk on her own. She had not realised how much her mother liked to chatter until she had watched the two matrons sitting, heads all but touching, for hours on end. Mama must have been starved of conversation these past few years and was making up for lost time.

The sound of seagulls settling to roost on the cliff face made her evening stroll quite different from one taken in Hertfordshire. Here there were no nightingales, at least not within earshot, but there were huge moths which flickered and fluttered outside the windows attracted by the many candles and oil lamps burning inside. There were bats also, these did not bother her as they might other ladies who erroneously believed the creatures would end up entangled in their hair.

Tonight she walked a little further along the cliff top path, the white sails of a grand yacht caught her attention and made her recall what Adam had said about buying such a vessel and taking her on board. The way she felt about him at the moment it was highly unlikely she would *ever* marry him.

She kicked a pebble, listening to it bounce down the cliff face before splashing into the water below. It must be high tide, the golden sand covered; one of the maids had been overheard by Lorna talking about smugglers using the beach no more than half a mile from here. Tonight there could be no nefarious activities, there would be nowhere dry to land the contraband.

It was time to turn back; she had no wish to be stranded on this narrow path, so high above the waves, when it became fully dark. She had walked no more than a few yards when a shape loomed ahead of her. Her mind was full of smugglers and she reacted without thought. With a stifled scream she turned and fled in the opposite direction.

Feet pounded behind her, she redoubled her efforts. Then her pursuer called out. 'Sarah, for pity's sake, it is I, Adam.'

She stumbled to a halt her breath rasping in her chest, not sure if she was more relieved that she was *not* about to be face to face with a smuggler, or angry that Adam had not had the sense to call out before scaring her half to death. A familiar arm encircled her waist and drew her close. How could she be cross with him when he was holding her so tenderly? His strong hands smoothed her back, he was murmuring reassurances, she relaxed against him.

'What possessed you to run off like that? Good grief, you could have gone headlong over the cliff. Who did you think it was, for heaven's sake?'

'I thought you were a smuggler . . . ' instead of sympathy his bark of laughter startled a flock of pigeons that had settled nearby. Shrugging off his arm she turned to face him, chin up and eyes brilliant. 'You have no cause for merriment, sir, I'll have you know that this coast is riddled with such villains. The excise men ride along this beach most days.'

Spluttering and hiccupping he mopped his streaming eyes with a handkerchief that glowed white in the gloom. 'I'm sorry, my love, I should not have laughed at your anxiety. But think about it, why should such men venture into the garden where they would be immediately seen? It's possible, but doubtful, that they might occasionally creep along the beach below us, but I give you my word, sweetheart, they will *not* be seen on this particular path.'

This was too much. How could he possibly know what went on? He had only just arrived; it was another example of his highhanded, arrogant assumption that he always knew best. 'You know nothing of the matter, you are not in a position to give any such assurances, and well you know it.' Her voice snapped like a whip and he visibly recoiled. She opened her mouth to apologise for her sharpness, but something quite different emerged.

'And another thing, Dr Moorcroft, how dare you ignore my express wishes and tell your mother that we are intending to be married next year? I'll have you know that when I return to Bentley it will not be to *your* home, but that of my employer. Our association will then be at an end.'

Aghast, her hands flew to her mouth as if she could push her intemperate words back. Far too late, the damage had been done. Before her eyes Adam metamorphosed from a laughing friend to an icy stranger, the love in his eyes replaced by something else entirely.

13

Adam viewed her through narrowed eyes. 'As you wish; I would not dream of holding you to an agreement you find distasteful. I hope when, in years to come, you're an embittered spinster languishing in the home of strangers, with no children of your own, you do not regret your decision.'

Sarah was at breaking point. This was all her fault; why was it that she behaved like the veriest shrew with Adam, but never with anyone else? She was an even tempered young lady, renowned for her good sense, yet she had been behaving quite out of character these past few weeks. Perhaps it was the death of Lottie that was making her so abrasive.

From somewhere she found her voice and managed to reply. 'I believe that making a promise is a sacred thing, I would have thought someone in your profession would understand that.'

'You made me a promise, you have broken that without a second thought. It is beyond me that you're putting the children of your employer before the welfare of your family.'

He was not family . . . what did he mean by this? He could only be referring to her mother. 'Are you saying that as we are not to be married my mother is no longer welcome at your home?'

He shrugged but made no answer to her query. 'I intend to continue my walk, Miss Shaw, I bid you goodnight.' Adam's expression was hidden as he had moved away from her. To her surprise he paused and spoke again. 'Do you wish me to accompany you to the house?'

She wished she had the courage to insist that he did so, but she was too bruised by his harsh comments and did not wish to break down in front of him. She did not want his pity. Shaking her head she turned and charged back the way she'd come. Surely if they truly loved each other this rift would be soon mended? She had made a tangle of matters; now her beloved parent would be obliged to go cap in hand to the elderly aunt and ask to be taken back. It was unbearable, Mama did not deserve such treatment.

There must be a way out of this disaster that would not involve her breaking her promise to the children, and would still allow her mother to live at The Rookery. At the moment she could not think of one, but she would pray that night for guidance, and forgiveness for her heartless treatment of the man who loved her.

★ ★ ★

The next few days passed without matters improving between her and Adam. He was scrupulously polite when in company, but ignored her completely if they happened to meet elsewhere. However he was a delightful companion to the children and to both his mother and hers.

Eventually she plucked up the courage to waylay him as he was heading for the stable. 'Dr Moorcroft . . . Adam, I must speak with you. We cannot continue to avoid each other in this way, it is giving rise to speculation and gossip.'

He was looking particularly handsome today, his riding boots polished to a high shine, his buff britches immaculate and his bottle green topcoat fitting his broad shoulders as if poured on to him. She loved the way his hair flopped across his forehead, refusing to stay in place.

'Well, I can spare you five minutes. What is it you wish to say?'

This was not an auspicious start, his demeanour was frosty, she almost decided to give up her quest for reconciliation and run away. 'Do you love me?' This was not what she'd intended to say and his reaction at any other time would have seemed comical. His eyebrows vanished beneath his fringe.

'I might ask you the same question.'

'I love you with all my heart. I cannot bear this distance between us and wished to know if you have changed in your feelings towards me.'

He rubbed his eyes and his posture became less rigid. 'This makes no sense. If you love me why did you reject me?'

'You frightened me by appearing so suddenly and my head was full of smugglers; I know that's no excuse for what I said, but when you laughed I lost my temper. It's not something I've ever done before, my words ran away with me. I have wished every second since that I had not said what I did.'

Still he remained aloof, but he was listening. 'Of course I love you, I shall do so the rest of my life. But I'm not prepared to wait on your whim. Either you agree to marry me next year some time or, however painful it is for both of us, our engagement is permanently dissolved.'

An ultimatum — how could he ask her to choose? 'Don't you see, Adam, I must put the needs of those girls before my own, before yours as well, they have lost so much and when Isobel is sent to school, will lose even more.' It was becoming more difficult to speak, her throat was thick with tears, but she would continue until she had said her piece. 'I love you, shall always do so, but I think it poor of you to ask me to make such a choice. I have given you my answer on that score.' She gulped and brushed the tears from her cheeks. 'Can I ask you, please, not to send my mother back? It would break her heart, and I think that your mother would be upset to lose her friend as well.'

His eyes were glittering strangely. Was he as moved by this as she? His voice was gruff when he answered. 'I never had any intention of sending her away, I'm not a harsh man. I respect your decision but think it's the wrong one. Children are resilient, where you and I will regret your decision the rest of our lives, they will have forgotten everything that's happened this summer in a year or two.'

'In which case, why are you not prepared to wait for that all-important *year or two*? If I recall correctly it was scarcely two weeks ago that you said you were prepared to wait indefinitely.'

'Did I really say that? I must have been insane; the more I've thought about it these past days the more convinced I am that we should marry next year. I have set in motion extensive improvements . . . '

Sarah barely restrained an urge to stamp her foot. 'I know, Mrs Moorcroft was kind enough to tell me. It is you that has reneged on the promise, not I.' She tossed her head. 'As far as I'm concerned I wish to marry you, but cannot do so next year. Is it your intention to throw away everything we have between us if you can't have your own way?'

The matter hung in the balance, then, Isobel called for Sarah to come at once as Beth had fallen and cut her knee. 'I'm sorry, I must go. Please give me your decision this evening when we can have time alone together.'

'I have made my decision. I want a wife who puts me first, loves me above all others. Either we marry next year or not at all; the matter is no longer open to debate.'

Not deigning to answer she hurried away to attend to her young charge. She had not thought of him as a selfish gentleman, but his intransigent attitude showed he could not be happy unless *he* was the centre of attention. In any marriage, as far as she was concerned, care for the children was paramount. A man who put his needs before those of his offspring would not make her a suitable husband.

Her head told her she had done the right thing, but her heart was broken.

The image he had predicted of her, being an embittered old spinster surrounded by other people's children, might well be a true one. As a governess she was unlikely to meet gentlemen of any description, and even if she did, she was in love with Adam, no one else could ever replace him.

★ ★ ★

Adam watched her go cursing himself for a callous, obstinate fool. His attitude, his unwillingness to compromise, had caused their love to be trampled beneath their feet. He was a rational man, not given to excitement or choler, yet he had behaved like a nincompoop. Small wonder she had stormed off in high dudgeon; she must believe him to be a person who changed his mind like a weathercock. He wanted her as his wife, loved her to distraction, had let his feelings separate him from commonsense. Of course he would wait, what he couldn't do was bear to be estranged from her in this way.

Tomorrow he would put matters right, humble himself and beg for her forgiveness. She was a remarkable young lady, as dedicated to her profession as he was to being a physician. He should have recognized this and respected her wishes, not tried to blackmail her into changing her mind. He was ashamed of himself, he couldn't face the accusatory stares from both matrons when they heard what he had said.

There was a horse sale being held a few miles away, he would take himself there and spend the night at a local hostelry. When he returned on the morrow he would begin to court her, to win her over and persuade her he was not the selfish dolt he appeared to be.

* * *

Sarah fell into bed that night exhausted by hiding her emotions from the ever watchful eyes of both Mrs Moorcroft and her mother. Fortunately the girls had noticed nothing amiss, and after a hectic day, both on the beach and in the woods all three of them had dropped asleep immediately. She had been too fatigued to look at her supper tray, knew she should be eating more, but emotional turmoil played havoc with her appetite.

The church clock in the village had just struck midnight when there was a thunderous knocking on the door. Tumbling out of bed, Sarah dragged on her dressing-robe, pushed her bare feet into her slippers and ran to the balcony. In the moonlight she could see a lone horseman standing in the portico, he had a leather satchel over one shoulder. She knew what it was disturbing their slumber. It was an express delivery.

Downstairs the housekeeper was busy opening the door. There was no sign of either Mrs Moorcroft or her mother, both ladies were sound sleepers, thank goodness. Such an arrival could only mean one thing, bad news of one sort or another.

The letter was handed over, the man did not wait for reply. Sarah could hear him cantering back down the drive moments after the delivery. With shaking hands she took the proffered paper. Stubbing held up the candles to allow the letter to be read. The name emblazoned on the front, in untidy black scrawl, was hers. She snapped open the sealing wax and scanned the contents.

Miss Shaw,
My carriage shall arrive at dawn tomorrow, my daughters and yourself will be in it. Taking my children away without my permission is indefensible. You will regret your rash decision.

This short note was signed with scrawl that she must suppose was the signature of Sir John. How had he discovered their whereabouts so soon? Adam had been so sure it would be several weeks before they were discovered. Isobel was not ready for the upheaval, her recovery was fragile, being dragged away from all those she loved best could prove disastrous to her sensibilities.

The housekeeper was waiting expectantly. 'It's from Sir John, the girls and I must return to Bentley immediately. I must wake up their maids and set them to packing. The carriage will be here in less than four hours. Mrs Stubbing, please arrange for a picnic basket to be packed. There will be no time to eat before we leave.'

'I shall see to it myself, Miss Shaw. Dr Moorcroft said he won't be back until tomorrow afternoon, I've no idea where he's gone or I would send word to him.'

Too late for that, if reconciliation there was to be, it must wait until the autumn when he and his mother returned from Dorset. 'I shall write a letter to Mrs Shaw, will you see that she gets it with her morning chocolate?'

Between them, Nancy, Jo and Betty

completed the packing, but not a moment too soon. The girls were half asleep; although dressed they had no ribbons in their hair or stockings on their feet. Such items could be added once they were on their way.

There had barely been sufficient time to scribble a quick note to her mother, as she and Adam were not on speaking terms she did not feel it appropriate to her to write anything to him. Nancy carried Beth, Jo supported Lorna whilst she helped Isobel to remain upright. The only positive aspect of this nightmare was that Isobel was too sleepy to understand what their sudden departure meant for her.

It was still an hour to sunrise when the coach left Poole. It was a sad squash in the travelling carriage, this one was not nearly as well appointed as Adam's had been. A blanket and pillow had been laid in the well of the carriage and Beth slept soundly down there. Lorna was curled up in Nancy's lap whilst Isobel slept in hers.

Soon the only sound in the carriage was that of deep breathing, outside the dawn chorus filled the air. It should have been an uplifting experience, but Sarah, the only one unable to resume her slumbers, hardly heard it. She was preoccupied with what was to happen on her return. From the tone of Sir John's letter it was quite possible she would be dismissed.

Although this would leave her free to marry Adam it give her no joy. The Fenwick household would be in disarray, it was scarcely more than a month since Charlotte had passed away. Lady Fenwick and Sir John were at odds and Isobel was in no fit state to be uprooted and sent to a boarding school.

She wanted Adam at her side, only he could give her the comfort she craved, but he was being left far behind, did not even know Sir John had found them. She prayed that when he returned later that day he would forget their differences and follow her post-haste.

* * *

The horse fair proved no more than adequate, no prime blood for sale; but what had he expected after all? Adam left the milling crowd and the overpowering smell of horse flesh and returned to his carriage. The urchin, who had been guarding it, held out a dirty hand and snatched the flashing silver coin from the air as Adam tossed it in his direction.

'Thank you, you've done a splendid job. Now, to earn yourself another silver threepenny bit, can you recommend a decent hostelry? The one in the village, The Nag's Head, is fully booked.'

The boy scratched his verminous head, Adam stood well back in case a crawler decided to change homes. 'Yes, mister, I reckon you would like the grand place what does the gentry. It's got an assembly room an' all.'

Directions were given and the promised silver coin exchanged hands. Adam had been overly generous, but the child looked as if he could do with a square meal. With the sixpence he could feed himself for a week.

Fortunately he was able to extricate his carriage from the others, leaving early was a sensible move. The narrow lanes surrounding the horse fair would be choked with like-minded gentlemen in an hour or two. The drive to The Queen's Head was accomplished in less than a half hour. No sooner had he drawn rein that an ostler appeared at the horse's head and a liveried boy threw open the carriage door with a flourish.

Adam had travelled without staff; one might have thought this would give the servants pause; but he was immaculately dressed, his team of matching greys superb — he was obviously a wealthy man despite his lack of attendants.

'I need a quiet room, with a private parlour, for one night only. Run and ask if such a thing is available before I climb down from the box.'

The boy tugged his forelock and

raced away to return with a beaming, rotund gentleman who was obviously the proprietor of the smart coaching inn. 'Sir, I have an excellent chamber at the rear of the building overlooking the gardens. It is fortuitous that you have arrived at this time, we will be fully booked by this evening.'

Adam leapt down and gestured to his carpet bag. 'I have correspondence to attend to, I shall require my dinner to be served upstairs.' The man nodded and bobbed beside him, extolling the virtues of his establishment, eager to impress his new customer. 'I shall want breakfast before I leave. I understand there is to be a cockfight tomorrow morning. Will it be held close by?'

'No more than a mile away, there's always plenty going on when the horse fairs are here.'

By seven o'clock that evening Adam had revised his plans. Although the landlord had provided him with paper ink and sealing wax they were inadequate for his purpose. The paper and pen were inferior and the ink so lumpy it made his handwriting rendered all but illegible. He would forego the cockfight, it had been a poor idea in the first place. Such spectacles no longer interested him, if he were honest, to see such noble birds tearing themselves apart was not a tasteful exhibition.

Tomorrow he would leave first thing, with luck he should arrive in Poole whilst Sarah was still teaching. Every morning between the hours of nine and eleven the girls attended to their books, after that she would be free to speak to him. The letter he had intended to write, pouring out his heart, offering his most abject apologies, could now be made in person.

His lips twitched as he sipped the last of his brandy. Both this, and the claret he'd consumed with his meal, had come from France. He was certain no duty had been paid on them. Thinking of this reminded him of Sarah's excuse for severing the connection between them; smugglers were obviously woven into the very fabric of life in these coastal areas.

★ ★ ★

It was a drive of more than two hours to his destination, as he left at seven o'clock he should arrive in good time. He was no more than three miles from the house when a flock of sheep blocked the lane and he was obliged to sit and wait for almost an hour whilst the shepherd and his mangy dogs returned them to the field. Never mind, he would now arrive when Sarah was finished her duties for the morning. He would return to his apartment and shave and change his garments before finding her. He patted his waistcoat pocket, a beautiful emerald betrothal ring had been waiting there for far too long.

When he guided his team through the arch into the stable yard he expected to be greeted by smiling faces, although only half the staff were from his own establishment, all in his employ were cheerful souls. Instead Tom Coachman was waiting to speak to him, his face sombre.

'Thank God you've returned early, sir, Miss Shaw and the girls have gone. A letter came in the night from Sir John, the carriage arrived at dawn, the house is in uproar.'

Adam bolted from the box waved his thanks and raced into the house. He could hear his mother crying in the drawing-room, presumably it was Mrs Shaw who was offering comfort. 'Mama, I am back now, tell me what you know.'

14

The miserable, rattling journey was completed in three days, instead of a leisurely five, they'd taken on the way down. However, it still gave Sarah ample time to dwell on the threatening tone of the note she'd received from Sir John. She was dreading the inevitable interview, certain he would dismiss her without references.

They had overnighted only twice and on both occasions the accommodation had been barely acceptable, and the food quite uneatable. Sarah only kept the girls' spirits up by constantly reminding them they were about to be introduced to their baby brother and see their beloved mama for the first time in many weeks.

The children became more animated when the carriage was obliged to wait whilst a colourful collection of gypsy caravans trundled past. 'I should love to live in one of those, it must be exciting taking your home with you, like a snail,' Lorna said, sinking back onto the squabs.

'So should I too,' Beth added wriggling to get between her sisters.

'I expect they are the same family as those that were living in Dr Moorcroft's woods before we came away. I expect they are on their way to the next village fair or market.' Sarah was glad of the distraction, it kept the children amused discussing what they'd seen.

All of them were heartily sick of the carriage by the time it turned into the drive of Bentley Manor half an hour later. It shuddered to a halt and three footmen appeared to open the door and collect the meagre amount of baggage they had with them. It was unlikely they would have their trunks for several days, the baggage cart could not arrive before then.

Isobel had seemed no more subdued than the other two on the long drive, she had made no mention of being sent away to school. If she *had* forgotten, then it was not Sarah's place to remind her and spoil the homecoming all three girls had been eagerly anticipating.

'Now, girls, stand still whilst you are tidied up; you do not wish to meet your mama looking disreputable.'

An unexpected call attracted their attention. 'My darling girls, I cannot tell you how much I have missed you. Come at once to the drawing-room; I have sent for your baby brother so that you may finally be introduced to him.'

The three girls glanced round to request permission. 'Run along, I shall see you upstairs later on.'

Lorna, holding tight to Beth, dashed off but Isobel remained behind for a moment. 'Miss Shaw, I have seen you looking at me most anxiously. Please, I have caused enough heartbreak in this family and I have no intention of causing more by making a fuss when I have to go to school. I'm just grateful papa has allowed me to return here in order to make my goodbyes.'

Sarah embraced the child. 'Sweetheart, how you have changed these past weeks. You are mature beyond your years, I pray that as time passes you will also regain your lively spirit. Off you go, Lady Fenwick is waiting on the terrace.'

With a sweet smile Isobel ran after her sisters. Was there something about Isobel's demeanour that raised suspicion? She was too sanguine, too accepting. Sarah knew she should be grateful there was not going to be a heartrending scene, but such an attitude was not natural. She shrugged, this was not the time to worry about this. It was just possible Sir John had changed his mind and Isobel might be allowed to stay at home after all.

Sarah remembered the curt note her employer had sent. This was not the missive of a man who had forgiven anybody. It must also mean her own removal from Bentley Manor.

The sooner this unpleasant interview

was over the better. She was in two minds whether to follow the maidservants to the side door or enter via the front. A noise alerted her and she looked round. To her astonishment Mr Burton, Adam's estate manager, peered through the archway that led to the coach house and stable yard.

'Miss Shaw, I was hoping to be able to speak to you privately before you go in. Do you think you could spare me a few moments?'

What on earth was he doing here? It could only be urgent news from Adam that had him skulking round corners in this way. Where could they go and not be observed? 'Quickly, we may converse by the home paddock, if we're observed, hopefully you will be mistaken for a member of the staff of *this* establishment.'

She led him to this deserted spot. 'Mr Burton, do you happen to know if Sir John is in residence?'

'He's absent on business today. I overheard a stable boy talking earlier, he's in London and will stay at his club tonight.'

'Thank goodness, that gives us a day's grace at least. I'm intrigued to know why you're lurking here, and how you knew I was expected this morning.'

'You know how it is, miss, word spreads quicker than wildfire from one estate to the other. One of our grooms is walking out with a housemaid here, so that's how I got this particular piece of information.' He stared across the lush green meadow; Sarah didn't like to chivvy him, he obviously had something of deep matter to impart.

'It's what I heard about Sir John. I know I should not be discussing my betters, but where it affects my employer and his future wife, I feel obligated to speak. Sir John is taking legal action against Dr Moorcroft, it's why he's in Town at the moment. He wants to have the pair of you charged with abduction.'

Sarah gripped the wooden rail in order to remain upright. This was dreadful news and explained the threat in the letter. 'I don't understand, Dr Moorcroft wrote to Sir John explaining why we'd removed to the seaside for a few weeks.'

'That letter never reached him. A man has been scampering all over the country, pretending to seek him out, in order to deliver it. However, the same girl who is supplying me with gossip knew where you were and she told someone else. When Sir John returned with Lady Fenwick it was no longer a secret and he never received the letter. I have it in my pocket, it only arrived here this morning and Sir John had already left.'

'Surely, when he does read it he will realise he has mistaken the situation entirely?'

'That's what I'm hoping.' He delved into his inside pocket and pulled out an impressive folded parchment. 'I thought if you gave it to Lady Fenwick, explained the circumstances, maybe she could be persuaded to send it by express to London.'

Sarah remembered the substantial amount of money she'd been given, that Adam had placed somewhere for safekeeping. 'Mr Burton, do you have access to Dr Moorcroft's study? Lady Fenwick gave me a substantial amount of banknotes, it's somewhere in the study. If you would bring that to me, Lady Fenwick would have sufficient funds to send as many express letters as she wishes.'

'I'll fetch it immediately. I'll be back within half an hour. Where shall I send it?'

'Hand it to the butler, make sure it has Lady Fenwick's name on the front of the package and that its not apparent what's inside the brown paper.'

It was imperative that she spoke to Lady Fenwick at once, hopefully the girls would be eager to rediscover their own possessions on the nursery floor and give her a few minutes alone with their mother. Pausing to straighten her bonnet and retie the bow, she shook out the folds of her travelling gown, checked the matching blue floral spencer was correctly buttoned and was ready to go inside.

The happy sound of childish laughter echoed throughout the house, it lifted her spirits and gave her the courage she needed. Before she could knock on the drawing-room door the officious butler, Anderson, flung it open and announced her as if she were visiting royalty. Scarlet cheeked she stepped in not knowing what her reception would be.

'My dear girl, how ridiculous. That man is a nightmare, but he's been here since he was a boy and it would be cruel to dismiss him now. Come in, we have been expecting you these past ten minutes. Let me introduce you to my son before he's taken back to the nursery.'

Isobel was sitting with the baby on her lap, Lorna on her left and Beth on her right all three looking thrilled with the new arrival. Dropping to her knees on the carpet, Sarah smiled down at the sleeping infant. 'He's so tiny; it's quite extraordinary but he already looks exactly like his papa.'

'See, Miss Shaw, he's got fingernails just like ours,' Beth gently spread out a little hand.

'He's perfect in every detail. Ah, here's Nanny to collect him and Jo has come for you three as well. I expect high tea has been set out upstairs. I shall join you shortly, make sure you save some for me, I could eat a horse this afternoon.'

Nanny carefully removed the baby and Isobel slid from the sofa. 'I could eat a whole cow all to myself.'

Not to be outdone, Lorna joined in the joke. 'Beth and I could eat an elephant between us, couldn't we, Beth?'

Laughing Lady Fenwick embraced them all in turn. 'I take it the food on your journey was not palatable?'

'It was absolutely vile, not like when we went down to the seaside,' Isobel announced.

'Never mind, darling, you're home now. Run along and have your tea, your beloved Miss Shaw will be with you directly.' Lady Fenwick's smile vanished as the door closed behind her children. 'My dear, you're in dreadful trouble. My husband has gone to the city to try and have charges brought against you and Dr Moorcroft. He would not listen to me, but then he never has. I was foolish to run away, I only made him more determined to snatch my darling Isobel from the bosom of her family.'

'Lady Fenwick, Dr Moorcroft wrote to Sir John explaining that he had advised we remove to the seaside for a few weeks as both Isobel and Lorna had suffered a severe setback in their recovery. A change of scene, somewhere that they could forget about their grief, was essential for their well-being. Unfortunately Dr Moorcroft's man, who was chasing after Sir John from place to place, was unable to catch up with him. Sir John has never read the letter.' Sarah handed it over.

'Good heavens! I can't tell you how pleased I am there's a simple explanation to your disappearance. I must send this letter on to Sir John immediately.'

Sarah thought this was not the time to remind Lady Fenwick that she had been the one to suggest that they flee from Sir John. 'Mr Burton has gone to recover the money you sent me, I did not spend any of it, perhaps the letter could be sent express using these funds to pay the exorbitant charge?'

'I had forgotten all about that money. I sold the jewellery I inherited from my own mama. Please, my dear, don't look so horrified. It was hideous, I had never worn it and I'm certain none of my girls would ever wish to do so either. They were mine to sell, and the money is mine to spend how I wish.'

★ ★ ★

The letter was enclosed in a fresh piece of parchment, a quick note explaining its provenance added by Lady Fenwick, and a senior footman was sent galloping to the nearest inn to send it on its way. Sarah was invited to the drawing-room once more. 'There, it has gone, now we can relax. Did you enjoy your meal, my dear?'

'Indeed, madam, it was quite delicious. I'm quite restored now that I've had time to wash and change my gown. Betty will have to launder the one I travelled in, it's unlikely the trunks will arrive for a day or two.'

'You always look as you should, no one could possibly fault your appearance. Now, tell me, what's this I've heard about you being betrothed to our handsome doctor?'

'It's quite true, my lady, however I can assure you, that unless Sir John wishes to dismiss me, I shall stay with the girls until they are ready to accept someone else.'

'Dismiss you? Whatever next! That will not happen, I can assure you. I've never seen the girls happier, Isobel is a different child. I know it's all down to your good offices.'

Sarah was glad this subject had been mentioned. 'Is she still to go away to school?'

'I fear so. However we have reached a compromise, and she's to go to the school that I attended, a select seminary in Bath. I have written to the principle explaining the circumstances and they will be most sympathetic.'

'Isobel appears to be resigned; I've told her that it's possible, as Sir John's grief lessens, that he might reconsider and allow her to return here for the holidays.'

'I should have said, that was part of the arrangement. Isobel will be allowed back next summer, unfortunately he will not budge on the Christmas and Easter vacations.' Lady Fenwick's face was sad, the thought of being parted from her favourite child for almost a year must be unbearable.

'You can exchange letters every week, it will be difficult for all of you, especially Isobel, but the months will soon pass.' Sarah realised no further mention had been made of her engagement, but at least she didn't have to explain she and Adam were no longer betrothed or the reason why this was so. Poor Lady Fenwick had enough to bear without burdening her with this.

'When is Isobel to leave?'

'She must be gone before Sir John returns. So she will depart tomorrow morning some time, Nancy can travel with her. She does not need to wait for her trunk, the garments she will require at school have been prepared in her absence.' She dabbed her eyes with a tiny embroidered square. 'I've arranged that she join me in my apartment after dinner, we have so little time to spend together and I think it will do no harm to keep her up this once. I doubt she will sleep, I know I shall not.'

* * *

The following morning there was no laughter anywhere, all the staff were aware that Isobel was to leave later. To her surprise the child had appeared in her riding habit. 'Mama gave me permission for a last ride around the grounds before I leave. I shall not be more than an hour, and Nancy has my clothes waiting for me to change into when I return. Would you like to come with me?'

'I dislike horses, as well you know, young lady. However, I should be pleased to walk with you to the stables and watch you from the terrace.'

In fact Isobel's pretty palomino pony was waiting at the front steps. The groom lifted Isobel into the saddle and with expert ease she rammed her foot home in the single stirrup and gathered up the reins. 'As I am to remain within the grounds, I'm allowed to ride alone this morning.' She clicked her tongue and the pony moved smoothly from walk to trot, to collected canter.

The elderly groom touched his cap and nodded to Sarah. 'Miss Isobel will come to no harm, she's like her pa, was born in the saddle. Them two's very similar, can't see why he don't see it himself.'

He stomped off, his disgust at the situation evident with every footstep. For all her past naughtiness, Isobel was obviously well thought of. Could it be this old family retainer had found the nub of the problem? It wasn't Lady Fenwick's love the little girl wanted, but Sir John's — and perhaps the more time she spent being spoilt by her mother the worse her relationship became with her father. Maybe he did recognize himself in his eldest daughter and was jealous of the attention she gave to Lady Fenwick.

What a muddle, and it was not up to her to put it right. She must pray that when Sir John returned he was more sanguine, had dropped the charges against Adam and herself. From the terrace she and Lady Fenwick, Beth and Lorna watched Isobel enjoying her final ride. It was Beth who drew their attention to what was happening.

'Miss Shaw, Mama, Isobel has gone. I can't see her any more, why doesn't she come back?'

Sarah scanned the grounds, in the blink of an eye the pony had indeed vanished. 'She must have ridden into the woods, is it safe in there, Lady Fenwick?'

'I believe so, I've never been in there myself. Look, isn't that Dr Moorcroft galloping down the drive? We can ask him to go and look for Isobel.'

Animosity forgotten, Sarah picked up her skirts and dashed down the terrace, around the side of the house so that she would be waiting in the turning circle when he arrived. There was something bothering her about Isobel's behaviour, about her appearance, but she could not put her finger on it.

She frowned and tried to recall an image of the girl on the pony. Good grief! Isobel had been concealing a package beneath her skirts. Her apparent acceptance had been a ploy, she'd taken this opportunity to run away and had taken some belongings with her.

Adam vaulted from the saddle, tossing the reins to a waiting groom and raced to her side. She didn't hesitate, she flung herself into his open arms. 'I'm so glad to see you, how did you get here so speedily? I'm so sorry we parted on bad terms, I love you and want . . .'

'My darling, I came to say the same to you. I saw Burton briefly and he explained the whole, don't look so distraught, we shall not be arraigned, I give you my word.'

'It's Isobel; she has run away on her pony. I should have realised how things were. She was too docile, too accepting. I should have been more vigilant.'

'This mount is fresh; tell me which way she went, I'll start looking. You must organise the outside men to follow. It's not a good time for a little girl to be abroad on her own. I doubt that you've heard, but there's been a spate of unrest in the vicinity. It would seem that there is a band of disaffected labourers; they started with just rick burning but now matters are escalating. We must find the child before she becomes embroiled in something unpleasant.'

Without further ado he was back in the saddle, thundering across the grass in the direction Isobel had taken. Large divots flew up behind him — he was ruining the lawn, but she was sure no one would complain in the circumstances.

15

Isobel had still not been found when Sir John arrived, mid-afternoon, in the expectation that his daughter would have left for boarding school. The house was in turmoil, Lady Fenwick red eyed from crying and Beth and Lorna clinging to Sarah's skirts as if their very lives depended on it.

Adam was still out searching, both the outdoor men from Bentley Manor and his own staff had joined in the search. Surely Isobel could not have gone so far that no one could discover her?

It fell to her to break the news to Isobel's father. 'Sir John, Isobel has disappeared. She went for a ride, with Lady Fenwick's blessing, this morning and has not been seen since. Dr Moorcroft has organised a search, but so far there's been no word.' She expected him to fly into a rage, to rail against the daughter who was proving herself to be disobedient yet again. Instead she watched him shrink, to age by ten years and he swayed as if he might fall to the floor.

She stepped in to support him, but he waved her away, forcing himself straight. 'Thank you for the information, Miss Shaw.' He surprised her a second time by holding out his arms to his remaining daughters; after a second's hesitation they ran to him to be gathered to his heart. 'Come along, little ones, we must go and comfort your mama. She will be distraught to have your sister missing in this way.'

'Papa, Bella has cried herself to sleep every night since you called us home. It's not going to school that is upsetting her. She thinks you do not love her and that is why she's run away,' Lorna said, staring up at him earnestly.

His expression was loving as he looked down at his child. 'It was wrong of me, she shall not go. I promise that when she returns home she will be welcomed, not chastised and we will be a loving family once again.'

Taking the hand of each he led them into the drawing-room. Sarah heard him reassuring the girls, telling them Isobel was no doubt hiding somewhere and would come home before it got dark. She prayed that was so, but with so many diligent men out searching she was certain that if Isobel *had* been hiding she would have been discovered long ago.

★   ★   ★

It was dark when Adam clattered back into the stable yard. He was all but done, his horse also. The only good news he could give Sarah, and the worried family, was that the rioters had left the area, Isobel was in no danger from them.

He dipped his head in a bucket of clean water intended for a stable, shaking the drips from his hair like a dog after a dip in the river, wiping as much grime from his face as he could with his handkerchief. There was little he could do about his appearance, but news was more important than sartorial elegance.

As he reached the side door it opened and Sarah stepped out. She was haloed by the candles burning in the wall sconces in the passageway behind her. Just the sight of her lifted his spirits, he loved her more each time he saw her.

'Adam, my love, you have no good news for us?' He shook his head, he remained at arms' length and she didn't blame him, he must smell appalling. 'I have been waiting for you, I think I know where Isobel has gone, but I don't think we should tell her parents.' She stepped out closing the door softly behind her. It was too dark to see her features clearly, but he could smell the sweet perfume of her lemon soap.

'Go on, darling, tell me at once where you think she is. We have searched everywhere, I would have expected to find her pony if she'd met with an accident, but there was no sign of him either.'

'I remembered that we saw the gypsies yesterday. I believe that Isobel has gone to join them. Sir John is devastated, quite overwhelmed at the lengths his daughter has gone to in order to avoid being sent to school. He has given his word that she may stay, but I fear if he's reminded about her first visit to the gypsies he will break his vow.'

'Good grief, we saw their fires burning a few miles from here. It did not occur to us that Isobel might be hiding in their camp. It makes perfect sense; however I doubt she's a welcome guest. Their chief will know harbouring a runaway will only bring unpleasantness to his group.'

'We must go at once and bring her back, I hate to ride, but on this occasion I shall put my fear aside.'

Adam's fatigue vanished. He would stay out all night if it meant he could bring a child safe home again. 'Then let's go, Sir John has a well stocked stable, I'm sure he can find something suitable for both of us. However, I must report to Sir John, tell him the modicum of good news that I have.' It was only then he became aware she was already dressed for riding.

'Fortunately the trunks arrived just before dark, I always take this habit with me even though I rarely use it. In my last employment I was obliged to accompany my charges on a morning hack.' She slipped her arm through his apparently unaware, or unbothered, by his rank odour. 'I am a competent horsewoman, albeit a reluctant one.'

★ ★ ★

Her earlier words were brave but she was barely able to control her knees from knocking. What she hadn't told him was that on one of these morning rides she had taken an unpleasant fall and this had given her a lasting fear of horses. His hand closed firmly over hers as if he sensed her fear.

'We must take some men with us, they can carry the lanterns. Don't worry, sweetheart, once you're in the saddle it won't seem so bad.' Somehow his arm had transferred itself to her waist.

'I don't expect you've ridden since having a fall, have you?'

'No, and I've no wish to do so tonight. I vowed never to ride again. My accident was caused by my mount's stupidity; having tossed *me* into a stone wall he bucked and upset the other horses which dislodged the young ladies I was accompanying.'

His rich, deep chuckle echoed down the pathway. Why was it he had this unfortunate propensity to laugh at her misfortunes? 'Tonight you shall overcome your fear; not all equines are bad-tempered, most are sweet natured and willing.'

They were greeted by the head groom. 'Going out again, sir? I shall come with you; how many more men do you want?'

'Two, and the most docile animal you have in your stable for Miss Shaw, she is a nervous rider.'

Far too quickly Sarah found herself being tossed into the saddle of an enormous gelding. The horse was an indeterminate brown colour, but had kind eyes. She sat rigid on the leather unable to move her boot into the stirrup. It was too far to the cobbles. If she fell from such a massive beast she would surely break her neck. Adam gently pushed her foot into the iron then checked her girth was tight; as he stepped back her mount's huge head swung round and gently nuzzled her trembling knee. It was as if he was telling her not to worry, she was safe with him.

Slowly her muscles unknotted and she leant forward to stroke the animal's neck. It was warm and solid beneath her fingers, she should have worn gloves but in her haste had not had the time to find them. 'Good fellow, I like you already.' With growing confidence she gathered up the reins and was ready to leave.

Adam moved his massive beast in close beside her. 'Are you ready? It's not that far, but we can't travel quickly now it's full dark.'

'I'm fine, you were quite right to tell me I would feel better once I was back in the saddle. This is the perfect mount for me, I'd trust him with my life.'

'Excellent, although he's a giant, he's a gentle one. Allow him to find his way, he'll not put a foot wrong.'

Sarah followed the lanterns bobbing like golden globes in the darkness, Adam riding at her knee. They didn't cross the grass or take the drive but left by the tradesman's track thus ensuring that their departure would be unnoticed. 'Lady Fenwick and Sir John believe that I've retired, with luck they will not notice my disappearance. I pray we shall bring back Isobel safely before dawn.'

'They were both distressed that the search was being abandoned for the night, but I reassured them that the only possible explanation was for her to have been taken in by someone, you would have found her otherwise.'

It became impossible to converse as the path they took prevented the horses travelling abreast. When the men leading the expedition pushed on into a gentle canter she discovered she felt more comfortable at this speed than she had at a trot. Her mount, his name was Bruno, had a rocking gait, his long stride making it the most comfortable ride she'd ever experienced.

She had long since abandoned any attempt to guide her horse, he appeared to know instinctively in which direction to go and where to place his hooves. Then, to her consternation the collected canter became extended; this was a dangerous speed and her old fear returned tenfold. Forgetting that Adam was riding close behind she tugged on the reins so violently that Bruno skidded to a halt blocking the path completely.

The gelding Adam was astride was forced to veer into the hedge in order to avoid a damaging collision. Whilst she maintained her seat Adam was not so fortunate and was catapulted headfirst into the hawthorn hedge. The men with the lanterns, unaware of the confusion behind them, had ridden on, leaving them in darkness.

She could not dismount without assistance, it was too far to the ground and she was racked by icy shivers. The gelding, unable to chase after his stable mates, stood restlessly beside Bruno. The commotion coming from the hedge meant that Adam was not seriously injured, it also indicated he was not pleased by being tossed into prickles for a second time by her foolishness.

His thrashing about was unsettling the horses, she must ask him to desist before she too was unseated. 'Adam, can you extricate yourself with less noise? Do you require assistance?'

The clouds that had been obscuring the moon drifted on just as his head appeared at the level of her knee. Her anxiety was replaced by concern, there was blood dripping down his face and one eye was closed. Without hesitation she kicked her boot free from the stirrup and swung from the saddle, her feet dangled in midair until she released her grip on the pommel and dropped heavily to the ground.

'Stay still, Adam, you are tearing yourself apart with your struggles.' The skirt of her riding habit was detachable, she unhooked it without a second thought. Now was not the time to be worrying about her modesty. Regretting the fact that she had not found her leather gloves, wearing them would make matters a little easier, she approached the hedge.

'What the devil are you doing? Sarah, the men could return at any moment, you must put your skirt back on immediately.'

Ignoring his protest she wrapped her hands in the folds of the material and then pushed aside the vicious thorns. 'This is voluminous enough to protect your face at least. Let me wrap it around you, then you can force your way out without further damage.'

His answer was muffled as he was already enveloped. Together they pushed and pulled until he emerged like a cork from a wine bottle. He cannoned into her and unable to keep her balance Sarah staggered backwards, bracing herself, expecting to be embedded in the hedge on the other side of the path.

But something solid blocked their fall. Bruno had placed his bulk between them and disaster. She was sandwiched between Adam and her horse, the breath squashed from her lungs by the weight. He recovered first, using the horse to brace himself he pushed himself upright. With a deft flick her skirt was swirled around his head and then back about her waist again. Not a moment too soon, as hoof beats indicated the imminent return of the menservants.

'Adam, I fear you will need stitches in at least two of those lacerations. I'm so sorry, I panicked when we . . . '

'It doesn't matter, darling, we should not have been travelling at that pace. I'm becoming quite used to falling into hedges when you're around.'

She tore strips from her petticoat and reached up to tend to his injuries. His gloved hand closed over hers. 'I can take care of this, it's not as bad as it looks. Trust me, I'm a medical man.'

His light-hearted remark made her smile. How she loved this man, he was perfect in every way. 'Who's going to put in the sutures? Even a man of such incredible ability as yourself might find it difficult to stitch himself together.'

The lanterns lit the scene like daylight. One of the men flung himself from the saddle and was beside Adam in moments. 'Is there anything I can do, sir? It were our fault, we forgot that

Miss Shaw was not accustomed to riding.'

'As you can see, Jim, I have stemmed the worst of the gore by this excellent bandage. It will do for the moment. Toss Miss Shaw back in the saddle and we will continue our journey. If I remember rightly the Romany encampment is no more than a mile or two from here; we should be able to see the glow of their fires shortly.'

This time Adam took the lead with one of the lanterns, Sarah behind him, the others relegated to the rear. They had not been travelling for more than one quarter of an hour when he called back. 'Wait, I can see riders approaching.' She felt a flicker of fear. 'Remain here, Sarah. Jim and Tommy come with me. George stay with Miss Shaw.'

She watched him ride forward fearlessly, always putting other people's safety first. The two groups met too far away for her to hear what was being said, and even the light from the lanterns was not sufficient to show who these other horsemen were. Then the strangers turned and cantered away, Adam trotted back to her.

Her eyes widened. He was cradling a small body in his arms, it was Isobel, it had to be. She urged Bruno forward, hardly daring to ask if the little girl was well. 'How is she? She's so still.'

'She's taken a nasty tumble, is suffering from a mild concussion, but her pulse is regular and her colour good. You were right, she *was* looking for the gypsies, it was they that brought her to us. It seems she put her pony at a massive wall and sensibly it refused and she sailed over it.'

'And Buttercup? Where is he? Is he not to be returned?'

He shook his head. 'No, I agreed they could keep him as recompense for their trouble. They had no notion where to bring her, but saw our lanterns in the distance and guessed we were searching for her. The loss of her pony is a small price to pay for her safety.'

The return was made at a faster pace

than their outward journey. Sarah was as eager as Adam to see the little girl safe in her own bed. Isobel would be devastated to have lost her pony, but perhaps it would teach her to think before she acted so rashly. The outcome could have been so much worse, she might not have been found, could have laid unconscious in the ditch until she suffered from a congestion of the lungs.

The house was in darkness apart from a light that shone in the study. Thank goodness, Sir John was still awake. There were grooms waiting in the stable yard to receive them, no one had retired down here.

She dismounted unaided and went to stand beside Adam. 'Hand her down to me, she weighs little, I can easily hold her for you.' Isobel stirred a little and her eyes flickered open. 'Sweetheart, you are safe now. Your papa and mama have been beside themselves with worry. They will be overjoyed to have you back.'

'Is Papa very angry with me? I should

not have run away.'

'No, you should not have. But that is in the past, the important thing is that you have come to no serious harm. Here, Dr Moorcroft is going to take you now and carry you inside.'

One of the stable boys ran immediately to rouse the household. Adam was still a few yards from the side door when it was flung open and Sir John erupted on to the pathway. There were tears streaming down his face.

'My darling girl, I thought you lost to me forever. Let your papa carry you in, your mama is waiting to greet you upstairs. I promise you things will be different from now on, you shall not go away to school but stay here with us.' He all but snatched the child from Adam's arms and still talking lovingly, he disappeared into the house leaving Adam and herself alone. A footman closed the door.

Sarah was upset that Sir John had not thought to thank Adam for rescuing his child, had not even noticed she was at his side. Relieved of his burden Adam swayed, if she had not steadied his arm, he might have crashed to the flagstones.

'My love, I must get you home somehow. You're in no fit state to ride, here, lean on me, I shall take care of you now.' Two of his own men arrived to assist her. 'I shall need a vehicle of some sort to convey Dr Moorcroft to his own home.'

'We have one waiting, miss, I'll take the ribbons. You'll be safe with me.'

★   ★   ★

It wasn't until dawn that Sarah was able to tumble into bed. Mrs Taylor had taken over the care of her master, proved herself adroit with a needle and thread and stitched him up as neatly as a parcel. The fact that Sarah was now sleeping in the apartment intended for the mistress of the house no longer concerned her. One thing this night had shown her was where her loyalties really lay.

She loved Adam, he must come first with her in future, but she still had the conundrum of her promise to the girls to overcome. She was too fatigued to worry about it, she must trust to the Almighty to provide a solution that would satisfy everyone.

16

Sunlight patterned the boards when Sarah finally roused the following day. It must be after mid day — how could she have slept so long without knowing how either Adam or Isobel were doing? Good grief! Lady Fenwick would be sending out search parties to look for her if she didn't return to her duties immediately.

The rattle of crockery approaching made her stomach gurgle in anticipation. It was far too long since she had eaten, she would break her fast and then ask for a bath to be drawn. Heaven knows what she could put on, all her possessions were now at Bentley Manor.

'Awake at last, Miss Shaw, Dr Moorcroft said to let you sleep.'

'Betty, what are you doing here?'

Her abigail grinned at her surprise. 'Lady Fenwick sent me, and your garments, as soon as she heard what had happened. Miss Isobel is wide awake and apart from a headache no worse for her adventure.'

'Is Dr Moorcroft well?'

'Right as ninepence, it was he that rode to the Manor to examine Miss Isobel himself and explain to her parents what had happened.'

Sarah flopped back on the pillows, he was stronger than she, had not let their night-time exploits get in the way of his duty. 'They must think poorly of me for deserting my post. I don't understand why my belongings have been sent . . . ' then she knew. She had been dismissed, hardly surprising in the circumstances.

Betty placed the tray across her lap, there was a dish of strawberries and fresh cream to pour over them, fresh bread and sweetly churned butter and succulent slices of pink ham. There was a jug of chocolate *and* one of coffee. It would be churlish to refuse to eat after so much trouble had been taken to provide her with her favourite things.

Her appetite returned once she began; she was munching her way through the last of the ham when the door opened. 'Adam, you should not be in here.'

Ignoring her half-hearted protest he strolled across and folded his long length on to a nearby chair. 'I think it's too late to think of propriety now, my love, after all I saw you in your petticoats last night.'

Her cheeks coloured at his unnecessary reminder. 'Kindly refrain from mentioning it, sir,' she said with mock severity. 'You look like a pirate with that eye patch. Is it to be a permanent addition to your ensemble?'

He chuckled. 'I sincerely hope not, my eye is not severely damaged, thank God. But I fear I shall carry the scars of my encounter with that hedge for the rest of my life.' He smiled ruefully. 'I hope that you will still love me now that I am no longer an Adonis?'

'I don't care about such things, as well you know. I have been dismissed from my post, I don't know whether I am glad or disappointed.'

His eyes twinkled and he stretched out and stole the largest strawberry from her bowl. 'You have misinterpreted the situation, sweetheart. Sir John and Lady Fenwick would keep you in their employ for ever, they think the world of you, as do their girls.' His lips twitched, he was hiding something.

'I hope you had nothing to do with this? I thought we had reached an agreement on the subject.'

'It was Lady Fenwick herself who suggested a solution. She wishes to spend more time with all her daughters in future, but is not in a position to educate them herself. She would like you to continue to teach them. However, not as their governess, but as their schoolmistress.'

Bemused by his statement, she shook her head. 'I don't see that there's any difference. What is it you're not telling me?'

'I must admit that *this* suggestion was my own. I thought you could set up a small, select, seminary here. We have dozens of empty bedrooms and as many unused reception rooms. My mother, and yours, are here to help with the teaching and running of such an establishment. The Bentley girls could attend as day pupils . . . don't you see? This way you can keep your promise to the children and to me.'

'My own school? Here? Oh, Adam, I can think of nothing I should like better. Are you quite sure you will not mind your home being overrun?'

'I'm looking forward to it. I told you before, I'm an enlightened man. I have no objection to you working as long as you put your family first.'

Sarah pushed the tray to the end of the bed and, with scant regard to modesty, flung back the covers in order to fling herself into his arms. 'I love you, Adam Moorcroft, I am the luckiest woman in the world.'

He wrapped his arms around her, drawing her close. 'And, I, Sarah Shaw, am the happiest man.'

We do hope that you have enjoyed reading this large print book.

Did you know that all of our titles are available for purchase?

We publish a wide range of high quality large print books including:
Romances, Mysteries, Classics
General Fiction
Non Fiction and Westerns

Special interest titles available in large print are:
The Little Oxford Dictionary
Music Book, Song Book
Hymn Book, Service Book

Also available from us courtesy of Oxford University Press:
Young Readers' Dictionary
(large print edition)
Young Readers' Thesaurus
(large print edition)

For further information or a free brochure, please contact us at:
Ulverscroft Large Print Books Ltd.,
The Green, Bradgate Road, Anstey,
Leicester, LE7 7FU, England.
Tel: (00 44) 0116 236 4325
Fax: (00 44) 0116 234 0205

Other titles in the
Linford Romance Library:

WITHIN THESE WALLS

Susan Sarapuk

When Annie revisits Chattelcombe Priory, it's inevitable that unwelcome memories are stirred. It's where she'd fallen in love with Edward, and where Charlotte's accident, which changed everything, had happened. When Edward returns to buy the Priory, he also attempts to win back Annie. But Tim, the vicar, wants to turn the Priory into a retreat centre, and Annie finds herself torn between the two men. Then, she discovers a secret, which changes her perception of the past . . .

THE AUDACIOUS HIGHWAYMAN

Beth James

When Sophie once again meets her childhood hero Julian, who's been sent home in disgrace, she feels that romance has made her life complete. However, her brother Tom and his friend Harry must confine Sophie to her home because highwaymen have been sighted in the area. Sophie, contemptuous of the highwayman rumours, finds that any secret assignation with Julian seems doomed to failure. Then — when she's involved in a frightening encounter with the highwayman — her life is changed for ever.